Hotels with Empty Rooms

Books by Harriett Gilbert

HOTELS WITH EMPTY ROOMS
I KNOW WHERE I'VE BEEN

Harriett Gilbert

HOTELS WITH EMPTY ROOMS

HARPER & ROW, PUBLISHERS
New York, Evanston, San Francisco, London

A Joan Kahn–Harper Novel of Suspense

FIRST EDITION

Library of Congress Cataloging in Publication Data

Gilbert, Harriett, 1948–
   Hotels with empty rooms.
   "A Joan Kahn–Harper novel of suspense."
   I. Title.
PZ4.G4645Ho3   [PR6057.I515]   823'.9'14   72-9768
ISBN 0-06-011519-X

Hotels with Empty Rooms

1

It had been his birthday and he had not noticed.

This upset him; it had never happened to him before.

He had been looking for some time at the calendar above the bar when he had seen the date and realized.

He had said in French:

—Hey, is that the date?

—Why, yes, had said the barman, who was the hotel proprietor's son.

Then he had wanted to say:

—It's my birthday.

Instead he had taken his drink to a seat by the large plate-glass window and watched the rain falling.

The hotel lounge was empty except for himself and the barman.

He knew that he ought to tell the barman that it was his birthday. If he did that the boy would smile and congratulate him, give him a drink on the house and when the others came down to dinner would tell them the good news too.

Then the Fincateau children would jump up and kiss him and Grand'mère would smile at him from beneath the shadow of her black hat and the middle-aged couple from Rouen would nod their heads at him from the corner table where they drank their nightly apéritif. Thus the day would be saved.

It was easy to watch the rain. It fell so gently here, not hitting the ground but brushing against it and trailing along it, dragged by the wind from the sea.

Two girls were walking along the road, hand in hand, their hair dark and flat against their heads, the collars of their oilskin coats turned up high at the back. They were young and not particularly pretty but he watched them all the same as they moved past him, their flat heads leaning the one toward the other, their bare brown feet kicking up the water in a fine spray.

And what would Miranda say if she knew that he had forgotten his own birthday?

She would find it amusing.

Had it not always been he who had been so particular about remembering things like that—birthdays, anniversaries?

He wondered if she had sent him a card. She might have. She did not know that he had gone abroad. Perhaps when he got back he would find it lying on the hall floor—a large, expensive card with nothing much inside it, just "Love, Miranda." On second thought he did not suppose that there would be one. It would not be correct now and Miranda was, above all, correct.

2

The girls in yellow oilskins turned a corner and were gone. He guessed that they came from one of the farms that crouched like dull gray animals in the fields behind the hotel. They had gone and only the pines were left to stare back at him through the glass. The wet road, the pines and, behind the pines, the sea.

Out there the deep Atlantic surged across rocks and the sound came to him through a glass window in which he could see his own face.

He went to the bar and asked for another whisky.

—What are we eating tonight? he said.

—Soup, said the boy. And langoustines and mutton with green beans.

—Ah, yes, it's Thursday, he said and smiled. It was always mutton on Thursday.

With his head he indicated the window.

—What filthy weather.

—Ah, yes, said the boy, shrugging his shoulders, lifting his hands palms uppermost to an unreasonable God.

—Did monsieur do much painting this morning?

—A bit.

The Fincateau children came downstairs. They appeared at the top of the stairs like red Indians on a horizon. With a whoop they charged toward him, legs pounding to keep up with their enthusiasm, brushed hair rising like spray from their heads.

—*Monsieur Winter, monsieur, comme on est heureux de vous voir.*

—*Où étiez-vous cet après-midi? On vous a cherché partout.*

They gripped at him with their hands.

—Calm down, calm down, he said. I couldn't play with you this afternoon. I was working.

—But it was raining. Were you painting in the rain?

—Of course not. I had some work to do in my room.

He had spent the afternoon lying on his bed smoking and reading in anesthetic succession two thrillers and one whodunit bought from the tabac down the road. He was not familiar enough with children to know whether they would understand this.

—Come, they said and coaxed him to the table where each evening they played a game or two of Pelmanism.

—You shuffle, Monsieur Winter, said the boy, the eldest.

—No, he said. You. You're much better at it than I am.

—Not Jean-Marc! cried the girls in unison. He bends the cards. Papa says so.

—Very well.

But he smiled at the boy as if to say: Women!

He shuffled the cards then spread them over the tabletop, face downward. His long, square fingers moved over the cards until each one lay in its separate place, untouched by another. The game was ready to begin.

—Where's Grand'mère?

—Here she is.

She came sideways down the stairs in the manner of old people.

He left the table and waited at the bottom of the stairs in order to take her hand and lead her to the table. Grand'-mère was a lady and a Catholic. She always wore a hat.

—Bonsoir, monsieur, she said.

—Bonsoir, madame.

4

He pulled a chair out for her to sit on.

—Hurry up, do, said the children.

Grand'mère took a long time getting settled. She was unbelievably bad at card games but she enjoyed playing. The children tilted forward on their chairs and drummed the soles of their feet along the crossbars. They watched the cards, looking out for the ones they knew: the queen of clubs with the torn corner, the creased four. Graham Winter lifted his glass of whisky to the evening.

Then the hotel proprietor's son went to the window and pulled at a piece of cord. Two heavy velvet curtains moved toward each other across the window until they covered it completely. He pressed a switch. A circle of artificial light fell from the ceiling and contained them like a cage. Or a playpen.

<hr/>

—Hey, Monsieur Winter! Give me another kiss!

—My sheet's come untucked.

—There's a mosquito on the wall. There. Above the washbasin.

He kissed the proffered cheek. He tucked the sheet in. He killed the mosquito.

—Now that's enough.

He turned out the light.

—Monsieur Winter, I've got a cough.

—Go to sleep. It'll be better in the morning.

—I can't sleep.

—Good night.

He closed the door and walked down the corridor.

At the top of the stairs he paused and looked down into the lounge, where the hotel guests sat waiting for it to be time to go to bed. They were not many. Apart from Grand'-mère Fincateau, who sat by the empty fireplace in a rocking chair reading a newspaper, there were only Monsieur and Madame Corneille from Rouen, Monsieur and Madame Bonnet, the hotel proprietor and his wife, and Giles Bonnet, their son.

Drifts of their conversations rose toward him as he leaned over the banister rail, feeling for the moment like a puppeteer or a god. Giles Bonnet was arguing with his parents about something. He was stabbing at the table with one finger in order to make his point. Graham noticed an unexpected small bald patch at the top of the boy's head and was once more reminded that today he was fifty. He decided not to go down and join them.

He turned away and went into his bedroom.

The window in his room was open. He closed it, taking his damp bathing trunks from the sill. Outside a white moon drifted across the sky behind torn clouds and the cry of an owl came to him from the woods along the skyline.

He hung his trunks on the back of a wooden chair and went to the wardrobe, which smelled of dry lavender. He took off his sweater and folded it before laying it on one of the shelves. He sat on the end of the bed and unlaced his shoes. As he leaned forward the blood rushed to his face and he could feel an uncomfortable weight against his forehead and his sinuses. He had to open his mouth in order to breathe.

On the inside of the wardrobe door there was a spotted yellow mirror and as he undressed he watched himself, noticing for the first time that he was developing a paunch, that the skin round his neck and chest was becoming white and crepey, that his thighs were woven with broken veins.

—Oh, God, he said aloud and he thought:

—Oh, God, Miranda. If you could see me now.

In February she, lying warm in bed while he was dressing, had said:

—You know, you've got a beautiful body.

She had said it as if she had never seen him before and he, unable to translate the emotion this caused him into words, had at first not said anything and then, feeling something was expected, had laughed and asked her what it was she wanted from him.

—Oh, very well then, be bloody, she had said, turning away.

He had never been good at accepting compliments.

Miranda used to say:

—You're like a man who crawls along on the floor because he's frightened he's going to be knocked down. For goodness sake stand up and be counted. Leave the crawling to people without legs.

—I don't want to be counted, he had said.

—You're frightened.

—Yes, I admit it. I'm a coward.

—Oh, for God's sake!

When she was exasperated she would clench her eyes shut and crush her forehead with the heel of her hand.

7

—You know what you've got? You've got a bad case of inverted pride, she had said.

—You deflate yourself so flat that it's almost as if you're crying out for someone else to come along and puff you up.

—That's not true.

He had been upset that she should think that.

—That's not true, Miranda.

Against the windowpanes the moths had begun their nightly battery. They came from the night with a burr of wings and a thumping of bodies to commit mass suicide against the glass wall of his room. He watched them for a while and then, instead of opening the window, got up and switched off the light.

In the room the moon reasserted itself. It picked out the sheets, the china washbasin, the canvases stacked one against the other along the wall. It picked out the whiteness of his body as he stood, naked, on the mat in the middle of the room. Although there was no one to see him he took his bathing wrap from the hook on the door and pulled it about him.

He lit a cigarette. It was strange, smoking in the dark. He could not see the smoke that he exhaled. He forced the breath down his nostrils for a long time to make sure that none of it remained in his lungs.

He lay back on the bed and took another drag at the crisp cigarette. This time the smoke hit a shaft of moonlight as it rose from his lips. He felt comforted.

—It's not so bad after all, he thought. Fifty. What's fifty? According to the Bible that leaves me at least another twenty-five years. One-third of my life still is live. Tomorrow I'll get up early and try to do some painting before breakfast.

He imagined himself striding along the glistening road to the rocks, his white shirt flapping across his back, his hair blown by the wind like a pine tree, like a sea gull dipping. He felt the smooth, varnished texture of a paintbrush between his fingers, the ease with which the paint would slide over the canvas.

He made himself think of these things, these good things, as men do when they dare not let their minds wander.

Later that night he heard a doorbell ring and the sound of voices in the entrance hall and on the stairs.

2

The next morning was a hot one. By nine o'clock the sun rode high and before the hotel, to the east, the sea was thick and calm. The sunlight ran over its back in ripples, a fine color like corn.

On the beach old women in black, their damp skirts hoisted above their knees, bent to gather shellfish. Graham watched them through the window of the hotel dining room as they glided over the sand scarcely seeming to move their legs, eternally crouching like the rocks that brooded over the headland.

He drank coffee from a bowl of Quimper pottery, he ate bread spread thick with white butter and apricot jam. The sun fell in through the window and warmed his hair. He thought:

—It's a good morning, and he said:

—Bonjour, madame, to Grand'mère, who, like him, breakfasted late.

The children were already down on the beach. He could hear their cries as they played with the waves at the edge of the sea or clambered over rocks to discover dark pools where green crabs hid and delicate plants shook their hair beneath the water.

He pushed aside the copy of yesterday's *Times* that he had been reading. He stretched his legs under the table. The cloth of his jeans pulled tight around his thighs. He breathed in and his shirt was drawn taut like a drumskin.

—You'll be out painting then, said Grand'mère.

—Oh, yes, he said.

She smiled at him and he smiled back, admiring the way she held herself so straight and proud even on holiday.

—You know we had a visitor last night, she said.

He wondered what she meant. She always spoke in mysteries, like a diplomat or a butler.

—A young lady. A young English lady.

With a rush the breath escaped from his chest and he sat up. In his mind an incredible hope formed and disintegrated so fast that he had scarcely time to feel the pain. He reached out for his packet of cigarettes and said:

—Really? A tourist?

—I suppose so, said Grand'mère, who had noticed.

—Just a young girl, she added. No one in particular.

She lifted a bowl of coffee to her thin lips and sipped, watching Graham all the time over the rim of the bowl. He said:

—I wonder what's made her come here, at this time of year. The season's almost over.

He asked:

11

—Has she come down yet? For breakfast?
—Not yet, said Grand'mère.
They turned to look at the staircase.

In the mornings Graham painted among the pine trees that separated the hotel from the sea. There he was well hidden from the curiosity of bathers and, besides, he liked the thick, cloying smell that hung in the air there and the way the unruly branches and needles framed the distant, quiet and dangerous sea.

Between the gray roots of the trees he would set up his easel and paint until lunchtime.

The hot day closed in upon him as he worked. All that existed for him then was the painting; the painting and its reflection. His narrowed eyes journeyed from one to the other, his strong, square fingers gripped the brush as it stabbed at the canvas or stroked it like a mother with a sick child. His body contorted itself over the easel. On his face unrecognizable emotions came and went.

As he worked the hot day moved above him and people died.

There was an occasion when Miranda had come into the studio to ask him something. She had stood in the doorway with a dishcloth in her hand and watched the labor taking place, not saying anything. The clock on the trestle table had ticked and the brush had dipped from palette to canvas and between them a time immeasurable had stood like guardian angels.

Possibly now she did not even remember the incident but it was then that jealousy had first been born in her. Graham had lost her then.

Women feel about love as men feel about war and the traitor must die.

Graham, of course, knew nothing of this. When she told him she was going he assumed that she was leaving him for another man and, true to his nature, had not put up a fight.

—You must do what you think's best, he had said.

—If this man can make you happier than I can then that's all there is to it. I'm sorry, I'm truly sorry things haven't worked out but . . .

He had sighed and smiled at her in a gentle way, ruefully. If Miranda was screaming at him to plead with her he did not hear.

So she had walked out of the door with her chinchilla coat and her matching pigskin suitcases. He had heard her feet click-clicking down the pathway, the iron gate slam. Five weeks later a friend had told him that she was married, to a man in the city by the name of Ford-Brown.

The glass doors of the hotel opened and a girl came out. She stood for a moment in front of the hotel then turned to her left and began to walk along the road by the sea, wearing stockings and a linen suit, holding her head straight.

She walked past the place where Graham was working,

13

past the shops and the café and up to the harbor, which lay round a bend at the far end of the village.

There women in black dresses and white lace coifs were selling bracelets made of sea shells and fishermen lolled beside the trolleys on which lay the remainder of the morning's catch: fat sardines swirling blue and silver in deep barrels, langoustines with enigmatic eyes, armored lobsters like captive knights and mussels with shanks of seaweed clamped between their lips.

On the water weekend pleasure boats bobbed beside the fishing yawls and to the east, on the other side of the bay, a ferry could be seen unloading passengers and a car or two, her great chains groaning behind her.

The village of Benmel stands on a stretch of shore where the Atlantic Ocean becomes the estuary of a river and so ten times a day a ferry crosses from one side of the river mouth to the other, from the wooded peninsula to the bulk of the mainland.

The girl went down stone steps to the harbor edge and stood there, straight, not like a tourist. Her hair was thick and white, her eyes were golden.

She looked across the water to where the *bac* was loading up. Cars and vans moved up the gangplank, soundlessly from such a distance. Gulls hung around the vessel. Men without faces moved to and fro on the quay.

The women who sold bracelets were watching the girl with their dark eyes.

She turned from the sea. She walked back a little way along the road to the hotel then turned up a path that led toward the woods behind the hotel. She followed the track

14

past farmhouses and thin dogs tied to their kennels until it petered out altogether and she was moving between trees.

She walked for a long time like this, fast, as if she knew where she was going.

She reached the pine grove at half-past twelve.

<hr/>

—How long have you been standing there? he said in French.

He had believed himself to be alone and then he had seen her, watching him. In the act of creation he was vulnerable.

—This isn't the bloody zoo, he said in French.

The girl looked to the left and to the right like a doe caught in a thicket. She was slender like an animal with narrow hips and small breasts set wide apart.

He said:

—Oh, well, it doesn't matter. I was just going in any case. It's feeding time for the animals.

He hoped she would smile.

She said:

—*Pardon moi, monsieur. Je voulais pas que . . .*

Her voice was soft and deep but he heard the English accent, the stumbling over words.

—Oh, God, said Graham. You're the girl from the hotel.

He laughed and, moving toward her, held out his hand.

—My name's Graham Winter.

—How do you do, she said.

It was an absurd meeting among pine trees, between an ocean and another people's land.

15

3

Graham spread cards over a tabletop and listened for footsteps on the stairs.

In and out, in and out went his fingers as he moved the cards until each one lay in its separate place, untouched by another.

A child said:

—You go first, monsieur.

The curtains of the hotel lounge were drawn. From the kitchen came the thick, Friday-evening smell of fish cooking and the sound of plates being piled up on trays.

Graham leaned forward and lifted a card. He turned it face uppermost upon the table. It was the three of clubs.

He heard the footsteps. He heard the slow, uncertain footsteps descending the stone stairway behind him. He turned another card, the five of hearts.

—Bad luck, monsieur, a child said. Now, Grand'mère, it's you to play.

16

The footsteps went toward the bar.

Grand'mère took two cards. She looked at them. She said:

—Why don't you ask her to join us?

She placed the cards on the table.

—Two tens! Two tens! cried the children. You've got a pair.

Grand'mère was watching Graham. He stubbed out his cigarette and pushed back his chair. He excused himself. He walked toward the bar.

He said:

—Madame Fincateau was wondering if you'd like to come and sit with us. We're playing cards.

The girl looked toward the table.

Graham thought that she must be a virgin to have a face like that, so strong and vulnerable with tight, inviolable lips and bright eyes that lashes shadowed at the outer corners. Her nose was large, her hair was thick and short. She looked as though she could have been a boy.

—And yet, he thought, if she were a boy they would say that he should have been a girl.

—You don't have to come, of course, he said.

—No, I . . .

—If you'd rather be left alone I quite understand.

He felt clumsy, like a bear trying to catch a dragonfly. He said:

—In any case, let me buy you a drink.

—No, please. I don't want . . .

—What?

—I don't want anything from you.

17

He was embarrassed. Taking off his armor he had not expected to be stabbed.

—Honestly. I didn't mean . . . Come on, let me, please. I'd like to. *Giles, apportez-nous deux whiskys.* You drink whisky?

She shrugged her shoulders.

—I'm really not trying to pick you up or anything, he said.

—Of course not.

She spoke as though she had taken his joke seriously.

—Well, then, he said.

They took their glasses and drank. Golden shadows flew into her face like a sudden bird.

—Would you rather have had a sherry or something? he said, placing his glass on the bar.

—No, this is fine.

He took a cigarette from his pocket and lit it. There was something he had been meaning to ask her.

—You'll probably say it's no business of mine, he said, but I've been wondering. What on earth made you come here, alone, at this time of year?

She was not surprised by his question. Nor did she answer it. She said:

—I've got to find a job.

He looked at her for a while, then said:

—Here?

—Not necessarily. Anywhere. I'm a bit short of cash at the moment.

—Oh. Well . . . What are you doing in France? Have you been hitching around or something?

She was wearing a beige linen suit with a cream-colored

blouse and low-heeled crocodile-skin shoes. Her skirt was too big for her. It hung from her waist in folds as though belonging to somebody else. She did not look like a hiker. She said:

—I just wondered if you knew where I could find a job, that's all. I don't have to explain myself to you.

She was angry but she did not raise her voice. She held it low and in control. He said:

—Of course not.

Then he had an idea.

—I could give you some work. Not for long but something to keep you going till you find what you're looking for.

—Doing what?

—Modeling for me?

In self-defense he had put the statement as a question.

—I can't do that, she said.

—Just your face. Nothing else. I'd like to paint you. Your face. It's interesting.

—Look, it's all right.

—No, please. I'd like to. Besides, you really won't find anything else here.

—Well . . .

—You said you needed money.

—I suppose so.

—How about it then?

She said:

—Well . . . Oh, O.K. Thanks. Thank you.

Graham finished his whisky and crushed his cigarette on the bar ashtray. He found the acts both of giving and of

19

receiving difficult to perform. He looked at the girl. He reached for her hand and changed his mind. He touched her elbow.

—There's time for a quick game of cards before dinner, he said.

4

There was a place where the headland thrust itself so violently into the ocean that the air was always thick with splintered water and the sound was of perpetual thunder.

Grass grew there in jaundiced scabs between the rocks and small blue flowers and trees with naked roots and malformed branches.

There the wind swept in low, bearing a crust of salt, and the sky hung near to the ground and the water was a long way beneath with ships and boats like flecks of foam as noiselessly they tacked into the estuary.

—Hey! called Graham. You're not frightened of heights, are you?

He had picked up a stone and was wedging it under the third leg of his easel to prevent it from wobbling. On his

21

back and on his neck he could feel the sting of the spray as waves crashed against the rocks that fell away behind him and the wind drove the broken fragments of water inland.

—I say! Judy! You're not frightened of heights?

The girl stood a little way from him with her hands in her jacket pockets and her feet placed wide apart.

—Why does it have to be here? she called.

—We can go somewhere else if you'd rather.

—I'm not frightened.

She came toward him and stood at the cliff edge. She said, more softly:

—I thought it was me you wanted to paint. I don't want to think you're just using me to be kind.

The wind was beating at her face, drawing her hair back to reveal a high, wide forehead, filling her eyes with tears.

—It suits you here, he said.

She shrugged her shoulders.

—Where do you want me to sit?

—Oh, anywhere. Not too far away though. I want to be able to see you.

The easel was steady now. He took his wooden box and from it selected a tube of burnt umber paint, which he squeezed into a fat, shiny coil onto the lid of the box. He took a brush and weighed it in his hand.

—Now, he said.

There was a moment's fear, a moment's hesitation, then, like a well-tuned engine, his mind and will and body moved painlessly into that other gear. His feet gripped the rocks beneath him, his back contracted over the awaiting canvas, his eyes narrowed to beams of light that thrust a straight and undeflected path through all the air and thought and questions that separated him from his subject.

It was a long time since he had painted anything but sea and trees and in his working now there grew a new excitement. In this solitary place the girl before him was a city to be besieged and he drove his battering ram at every gate and fissure. He assaulted the amber eyes, the large nose with its curved nostrils, the full, hard lips, the place above the ears where short white hairs fluttered like uneasy pennants against an otherwise immobile face.

The brush that was an extension of his hand stabbed at the canvas. His breath came hot and slow, drying his lips.

—Come on, he muttered.

And:

—That's it. That's it.

While all the time the girl sat still like a city with many walls that is impregnable.

After a while he took the painting from the easel and, resting it on his hip, circled around her, treading over the blue flowers and the grass that was sticky with salt, realizing that he was getting nowhere. There was something about this girl that he could not understand and, not understanding, could not hope to reproduce.

He stood in front of her. She was looking out over his shoulder to the sea. Her eyes were like gold, and amber, and yellow glass with the sunlight reflected on them. Graham was no longer painting, only watching her and waiting.

He thought:

—How old is she? She can't be more than eighteen,

nineteen. She's young and alone with her soft, deep voice and her strange clothes and her . . . What is it?

He thought:

—Something almost like serenity.

Something so close to serenity that for a while he had been deceived into thinking that that was what it was.

He looked at the painting again: the mass of lines and shadows that added up to nothing. Again he looked at the girl with her still, bright eyes. Then he remembered.

There had been a dog once, Miranda's dog, and one day it had got out into the road and had been hit by a lorry. They had heard the brakes screeching and when they had got out there the driver was standing on the pavement with something in his arms.

Miranda had said:

—You've killed him.

—Poor little bugger, the driver had said. He's not quite gone yet.

Graham could see the lorry with its crazy front wheels up on the pavement. He saw the driver in his overalls and red checked shirt. He saw the dog, the dog's eyes. They were large and quite opaque.

Graham walked across the rocks to the easel. With extreme care he propped the canvas up against the easel, not looking at the painting. After a while he said:

—I think we'd better stop now, Judy.

He heard the girl get up and come toward him.

—What's the matter? I wasn't at all tired. Did I move too much?

24

—I've just . . . No, it's all right. I was just thinking of something else.

He felt her come round in front of the easel and look at the painting. He said:

—It's hardly started yet.

She said:

—It's good.

—Thank you.

He looked at her. He said:

—I think perhaps . . .

—You don't want to go on.

—It's not that.

—Was I terrible? It's the first time.

—You were fine, he said.

He pulled from his pocket a flattened pack of cigarettes and handed her one and then he took one for himself and lit it, with his hands cupped around the unsteady flame. When it was alight he passed it to her.

—You'd better light yours from this. The wind . . .

He watched as she dragged on the cigarette, drawing the smoke deep into her lungs, like a man.

—Listen, he said. If I'm going to paint you . . .

—Yes?

He did not know whether he would be able to explain the thing inside him, not understanding it himself, but he said:

—If I'm going to paint you I've got to know more about you. It just won't work like this. People, you see, they're not like landscapes or . . . I don't know. You can't just take them and fill them with yourself. You've got to find out what's

25

really there. The truth if you like. You, for instance . . . I mean, what's going on inside you? What are you thinking? I don't know. All I can see is flesh and skin and hair. A sort of mask. I just don't know.

—I see, she said. I suppose there had to be a catch.

—I don't understand.

—It doesn't matter.

—But it does. To me. You're hiding such a lot. There's something . . .

He wanted then to take her by the shoulders and shake her until something snapped, until some truth burst through.

Perhaps there was something in the place that demanded it, some eternity in the rocks and in the moving ocean that showed him for a moment the lie that was his painting, that was the girl. He wanted to make her cry.

—Please stop questioning me, she said.

—I've got to know.

—Leave me alone.

She started to walk away from him.

Without giving himself time to think, Graham grabbed the sleeve of her suit and pulled her back.

—You're not going like that.

She turned to face him and he saw to his relief that he had nearly won. Her cheeks were flushed and when she spoke there was a crack in her voice.

—Let go of me, you sod.

—Not yet.

She lunged at him with her fist and for a moment he staggered, letting go of her arm. She was strong.

26

She started to run away from him, over the rocks. He caught up with her and pulled her round to him again. She flung herself against his chest, hitting at him, and then with a gasp she began to cry.

He held her to him. Her tears were warm through his shirt. He could feel the brittle cage of her body shaking.

5

Later Graham was able to say:

—It wasn't my fault.

He was able to believe this later.

Then, however, in that moment when the girl cried because he had made her cry, when she clung to him because he had made her weak, he was frightened and this fear, this guilt engendered by having dared to alter the course of events, was to color everything that happened subsequently.

Graham, passive Graham Winter, whose inability to make decisions had so infuriated Miranda, whose life, whose career, was composed of a series of lucky, unasked-for accidents, had stepped out of character.

He did not realize that character is the result of what one does, not the other way round. That he did not realize this was part of his character.

What did happen subsequently was therefore inevitable

and when, as he did, Graham was later to deny that anything really *had* happened, he was perhaps not far from the
truth.

***

The girl had spoken first. She had stood back from him
so that he had seen that her face was red, that her eyes were
swollen, and she had said, wiping her nose:

—I'm sorry. I didn't mean that to happen.

—Nor did I, he had said. Shall we pretend it didn't? Can
you do that? In any case it was nothing personal. Nothing
to do with you, if you see what I mean.

He tried to laugh.

—If you'd have been a bowl of fruit I'd have probably
chucked you across the room. Do you understand?

—Yes. Of course.

He had wondered if she did. He had hoped she did. She
had certainly looked calm again. He had, however, decided
not to test her; or himself. He had said:

—I still think we'd better not carry on for the moment.
We'll start again tomorrow. How about that?

—That's fine.

She had helped him gather up his easel and his paints
and together they had walked back to the hotel for lunch.
The salt wind had followed them inland as they went. That
had been on Saturday.

***

On Sunday they went down to the beach to work.

This time Graham painted steadily and fast without thinking too much. The results were satisfactory. He was a gifted artist, not a genius. He knew that. He did not need to lose his temper or be unpleasant to people in order to create. The scene of the previous day had been a conscious indulgence, unnecessary and not to be repeated.

As he worked, with eyes narrowed, his lower lip clamped between his teeth, Graham was content.

At noon the sky clouded over. A black shadow swept in across the sea and up the beach. Feeling the cold, Graham said:

—We'd better go in.

She came to him.

—Was I O.K.?

—You were fine.

She did not ask to see the painting and he was glad.

They walked up the beach together. Ahead of them the gray pines leaned to the wind. He said:

—I think it's going to rain.

They walked slowly because the sand was soft under their feet.

Judy said:

—What'll you do this afternoon, if it does rain?

—I don't know.

For some reason he was afraid that she might ask him to go into town with her or something but she did not. She walked beside him looking straight ahead, asking for nothing. Graham was amused at the warmth he felt inside him for the way she walked.

They crossed the pine grove and the road and went into the hotel lounge. It was not yet time for lunch.

—What'll you have to drink? he asked her.

—Nothing, she said. No. Really.

—Come on now.

They smiled at each other. Now it was a joke they shared.

—Whisky? That'll warm you up.

—Could I . . . ? Do you mind if I have a glass of wine instead?

—Of course not. Giles!

The boy came from the kitchen and served them. He asked, in French:

—Did monsieur do much painting this morning?

—Not bad. Not bad.

—And mademoiselle? Is she a good model?

He smiled at Judy and Graham noticed how white the boy's teeth were, how thick the black, curled hair that helmeted his forehead. He said:

—She was fine, thank you.

—What did he say? asked Judy.

—He wanted to know if you were a good model.

—What did you tell him?

—Never you mind. Drink this.

Madame Bonnet called from the kitchen. Before the boy went to her he said:

—Oh, Monsieur Winter, I almost forgot. Your paper. You didn't take it this morning.

He reached under the counter and handed Graham a folded copy of yesterday's *Times*.

—Thank you, said Graham.

He spread the paper over the bar.

—Well, he said after a bit, I don't know why I bother. The same old stories. Unemployment, strikes, protests, murders, rapes. Various members of the royal family in various hats.

He smiled and turned to Judy. Then he said:

—What's the matter?

She said:

—Nothing.

—You look upset. Is it something I've said?

—Of course not. It just never occurred to me that you'd get English papers here.

She paused.

—What day is it today?

—Sunday. Didn't you hear the church bells this morning? Not even the infidels are allowed to rest in peace on Sunday.

—Can I read your paper?

—It's not today's. I get them a day late.

—Oh, she said. Well, that doesn't matter. Do you mind?

—Be my guest.

He pushed the paper to her along the bar. He watched her reading it, hugging it to herself like a girl might do in an examination when she does not want her neighbors to copy her answers. He thought:

—I mustn't ask her anything. No questions. That way we'll be all right.

He took his whisky and drank. After a while she pushed the paper back to him.

—Thanks, he said. Well, it looks as though it's almost lunchtime.

In the lounge behind them several people had gathered: families from the village who came on a Sunday to eat at the hotel. There were stout, red-faced men in black berets and girls with orange hair and children and youths uncomfortable in their starched collars and elderly spinster aunts in gray lace blouses who sat in corners waiting to turn young men into pigs.

Madame Bonnet came out of the kitchen and ushered them all into the dining room.

The Fincateau children came downstairs with Grand'-mère. They wore blue turtlenecked sweaters and lace-up shoes with thick soles. They ran to Graham and said:

—Do come and eat with us. We haven't seen you for such a long time. You weren't in church this morning. Do eat with us, do.

—Leave him alone, said Grand'mère. He probably wishes to sit with mademoiselle.

She inclined her head toward Judy, like a duchess.

Graham said:

—That's all right. We'll all eat together.

The dining room was noisy with people who had cleared their consciences with their God.

The food, when it arrived, was splendid. Bowls of steaming vegetable soup were followed by mussels in a garlic sauce. Then came slices of pink beef and fried potatoes and salad tossed in vinegar and oil, then Camembert and Port-Salut and pears and grapes and custard cakes and café filtre so hot it burned the tongue. The gentlemen filled the air with the smoke of their cigarettes, the ladies sipped cognac, the children dropped their knives and screamed and hit each other with their napkins.

And it rained.

All the afternoon it rained. Not in drops but in a blanket that covered everything, filling the canvas seats of chairs that stood outside the hotel, churning the gravel patio to alluvial mud, dislodging from the gutters twigs and birds' nests that had remained there, undisturbed, all summer long.

The villagers were resigned.

—Summer is over, they said. *Tant pis.* So much the worse.

They moved into the lounge, some to sleep, some to talk. Madame Bonnet brought some more coffee. The children fretted. They ran up and down the stairs, they blew on the windowpane and drew pictures in the condensation, they asked:

—When will it stop? When can we go out to play?

Graham went to his room and he locked the door. He closed his window. In the fields behind the hotel he could see cows standing together with steaming bodies and dull faces. He mopped up the water that was in a puddle on the floor beneath the window. He took off his shoes. He lit a cigarette. He found his book and opened it at the page with the bent corner. He lay on his bed and read.

On Monday, shortly after four o'clock in the afternoon, it stopped raining and Judy said:

—Let's take the children for a walk, shall we?

They were in the hotel lounge. Graham was doing the Sunday *Times* crossword puzzle. He was thinking:

34

—Someone read my paper before me this morning. A newpaper can never be successfully refolded once it has been read. It must have been her. Why, though? What is she looking for?

He took his pen out of his mouth and said:

—Yes, let's. Where are they?

—Upstairs. We've been playing consequences.

—In French?

She laughed.

—No. Picture consequences. You know. You all draw a head, then fold the paper back so that only the neck shows and the next person does the body. Well, I used to play it when I was younger. Not professional enough for you, of course.

—Nonsense, said Graham, feeling jealous.

—Come on, he said. Let's call them.

He went to the stairs and called:

—*Jean-Marc, Annie, Catherine! Venez! On va se promener.*

The children came. The girls took hold of Judy, one by either hand, and off they set. Jean-Marc and Graham walked a little way ahead.

The road was still wet from the storm. Drops of water hung from the pine needles and fell from time to time onto the pitted sand beneath.

—Where shall we go? the girls asked.

Judy said:

—What do they want?

—They want to know where we're going. What do you suggest?

—How about the headland?

—I don't think so.

Was she trying to exorcise ghosts?

—It's dangerous there, he said.

—Nonsense. It'll be fun. They're not babies, are you? she said.

She smiled at the girls and they smiled back. They did not understand what she had said.

—Very well, said Graham.

They turned left and climbed over rocks for a few minutes until they reached the promontory. Around them, below them, the sea thundered and broke. Gulls and cormorants flew low, calling in shrill voices, and the salt that was in the air lay thick on their skin and on their lips. Although the rain had stopped it was not warm.

—What now? said Graham in French.

—A game! cried the children. A game!

—What sort of game?

—Tag, they said. You have to try and catch us. Count ten to let us get away.

—I don't know, he said. You'll have to be careful. The rocks are slippery and we don't want . . .

—Oh, come on, they said. All right then, *you* try and catch us, mademoiselle.

—No, said Graham. It's all right. I'll be It. One, two, three . . .

The children ran from him, screaming with delighted fear. Judy ran with them.

. . . seven, eight, nine, ten. I'm coming!

Graham decided that he would catch Judy first. That would be the fairest thing to do. He started toward her.

She saw him coming and waited until he was almost up to her, then, at the last moment, veered away so that he lost his balance.

—Just wait! he cried. I'll get you!

He turned and they were all four running from him, inland. The children still screamed. Their voices were thin and clear above the bluster of the wind and the crashing of the waves below.

—I'll get the lot of you! he cried.

And he too began to run. He had almost caught up with them when Jean-Marc said:

—All right! Let's split up!

And turned once more toward the cliff edge.

—No! Graham called. Come back!

He went after the boy, who only ran all the faster.

—Jean-Marc! Please! Be careful! he called.

Then Judy yelled:

—Jean-Marc!

Hearing her voice, the boy stopped but it was too late. The crepe soles of his sandals were small protection against the slippery surface of the rocks. He skidded several feet, then fell and would not stop falling.

On the ledge he looked like a discarded puppet and his sisters watched him without tears.

Graham said:

—Judy, take the children away from here. I'm going down.

She did not hear him. She came past him and knelt at the cliff edge. Then, taking the entire weight of her body with her elbows and hands, she swung herself out into space.

She hung for a moment until her feet found a wedge of rock on which to rest, then she let go with her left hand and felt about for some new protrusion to hold onto, lower down.

Having found this, she allowed her feet once more to drop so that once more she hung by her hands alone. Her wrists, Graham noticed, were strong like bands of steel.

Thus she descended the rock face to where the boy lay. Graham did not try to stop her nor did he try to help her. He only watched.

It took twenty minutes in all for her to get down there. When she reached the body she said:

—He's alive.

After that it was easy. A quick sprint back to the hotel, telephone calls to the hospital, the gendarmerie, the coast guard, questions asked and questions answered, tears and prayers and hysteria—the aftermath of any accident.

Graham lived through it all as though it were not happening. As soon as he could he went to his room and vomited into the washbasin. It took a long time for him to bring up everything that was inside him.

When it was done he lay on his bed and shut his eyes.

The last thing he saw before he slept was a pair of hands with wrists that were strong like bands of steel and the hands were holding a newspaper, tearing a newspaper, tearing it into a million shreds that fell like rain against the back of Graham's mind.

6

—The boy's parents have asked me to say that if there is any way in which they could express their gratitude to the young lady . . .

—No, no, said Graham. I'm quite sure that mademoiselle won't want any fuss.

—I see, said the policeman. Of course.

He was a young man, plump, with pink skin and eyes like gimlets. All the time he spoke he looked round the room, searching for possible clues to as yet uncommitted crimes. Occasionally he looked toward the stairs.

—Mademoiselle is still sleeping, said Madame Bonnet, who was dusting the bar. She is not to be disturbed, poor dear. She's very tired.

There were only the three of them in the lounge: Graham, the policeman and she.

When Jean-Marc's parents had been telephoned at their Paris flat and told of the accident they had set off immediately, arriving in Benmel at ten o'clock at night in a large black car with a chauffeur. They had collected Grand'mère and the children and had taken them with them to a hotel in town in order to be nearer to the hospital.

—I see, said the policeman again.

—Of course mademoiselle must be allowed to sleep.

—But the boy, said Graham. You are sure he's going to be all right?

—Oh, yes, said the policeman. Children, you know, they're indestructible.

He sounded sorry.

—Bruises and cuts, a fractured collarbone, nothing that time won't mend. There wasn't much blood lost either, thanks to the young lady.

He ran his hand over his hair so that it lay even more smoothly and sleekly against his head, then he said:

—Though, of course, it *was* quite unnecessary.

—What was? said Graham.

—For her to have done what she did, to have climbed down there. The coast guard are trained for that sort of thing. We could have had two accidents on our hands.

—No, said Graham. Well, I daresay she didn't think about that. You see, for all we knew the boy could have been . . .

—Of course, said the policeman.

He sat well back in his chair. His pink hands rested on the kepi in his lap.

Madame Bonnet came round from behind the bar and began to dust the table at which they sat. Possibly by accident she brushed some cigarette ash into the policeman's lap. The policeman stood up.

—Well, he said. I mustn't waste any more of your time. Or mine.

He put on his hat.

—Good day, Madame Bonnet. Monsieur Winter. Perhaps we shall meet again.

—Perhaps, said Graham.

The policeman went. Graham watched him through the window as he walked to his car. When he reached the car he stopped and turned back. His eyes met Graham's through the glass.

—What is he looking for? thought Graham.

The policeman got into his car and drove away.

—Is he gone?

—Yes.

—Well, that's a relief.

Madame Bonnet tucked the duster into the waistband of her apron and sat down in the chair that Graham had vacated.

—I never trust them myself, she said.

Through the window Graham watched the untidy clouds that trailed overhead. They moved slowly, inexorably, without apparent purpose.

—I got the impression that he didn't trust us much either, he said. As if we had something to hide.

—That's just their way. And then we all have our little secrets.

—You, madame?

—Oh . . .

She fluttered her hand to indicate the insignificance of whatever skeletons she might or might not be harboring.

41

She was a practical woman with a square jaw and thick red legs.

—I don't think that I have, said Graham. No, I really don't think I have.

—Well . . . , she said.

She did not believe him.

Judy stood at the top of the stairs.

—Has he gone, then? she said.

—Yes.

—I thought I heard a car drive off.

Graham said:

—You were asleep.

Madame Bonnet said:

—I'll get you some breakfast, dear.

—I thought you were asleep, said Graham.

—No.

She came down the stairs.

—I just didn't want to see him.

She sat at a table.

—You do understand, don't you?

—I suppose so.

She looked tired. Her face was white and red in patches, her eyes were bright. She asked:

—Have the papers come this morning?

—I suppose so. I haven't had time. The policeman . . .

—Oh, yes. What did he say?

—About the boy . . .

—What? He's all right?

—Yes. A fractured collarbone. Nothing serious. He didn't even lose much blood, thanks to you.

—Well, that's something.

—Yes. Judy, I'd like to tell you how . . . really, how . . .

He paused and looked at her. He saw that she did not want him to continue.

—In any case, he said, and handed her a cigarette. She held it with her lips while he lit it then closed her eyes and dragged the smoke into her.

There were gulls crying and clouds like chicken feathers across the sky.

Madame Bonnet brought a bowl of coffee that was warm and gray with flecks of boiled milk moving across the surface. The girl said:

—So they've gone. The grandmother and the girls. They've left.

—Yes, said Graham. The parents came from Paris. They all went up to Quimper to be nearer the hospital.

—I see.

She looked at her coffee, watching the white flecks circling on the surface. The skin under her eyes was swollen but she wore her makeup bravely—the improbable black lashes, the pink lips.

—How easy to be a woman, Graham thought. To wear a public mask over the private mask like a game with many mirrors.

He said:

—So there's only the two of us left, now that the Fincateaux have gone.

—What about the others? You know.

—The Corneilles? They went yesterday. Sometime in the afternoon. Probably while we were out.

43

—Graham, she said.

She called him Graham. It was not often that she used his name.

—Yes?

Together they extinguished their cigarettes in the ash-tray. He saw her hand like . . .

She said:

—How long do you think it'll take, to finish the painting?

—I don't know, he said. Why?

—Could you—I mean would it be possible for you to finish it off today?

—Today?

—Yes, she said. Would it?

—Well, I could. I could do it. I could finish it off later, from memory.

—Would that muck it up completely?

—No, he said.

Then:

—Look. Is it the money? I can easily pay you now for the work you've already done and then . . .

—It isn't that. Of course I'll need the money, what I've earned, but it's not that.

—What then?

—I've got to go. I want to go tonight.

Graham felt as though she had hit him. But not in the face. Or rather, not even as though she had hit him but as though her words had triggered off some pain that he had known before and for which familiarity had not bred contempt. He said:

—I see.

His cigarette in the ashtray had not gone out. There was a smell of burning filter. He said:

—I suppose you never meant to stay for long.

—I'm sorry, she said.

—No, please . . .

—I've just got to move on.

—Where will you go to?

—I don't know.

Graham looked at his watch. He did not see what time it was but still he said:

—We'd better get to work then.

—Graham . . .

—Yes?

He had chosen to sound irritated.

—Please, I really am sorry. Especially when you've been so awfully good to me.

—I haven't done anything.

—You might not think you have.

—I haven't. You've worked for me, I'm paying you.

—Not the money.

—Not anything.

—All right, she said.

—You're your own mistress. If you want to go, then that's all there is to it. I'm sorry, of course, but . . .

Then he stood up.

—I'll go and get my paints. We can work down here. We won't be disturbed now and it's pretty miserable outside.

He started for the stairs and saw that there was something lying on the bar. It was his newspaper. He picked it up. The girl said:

45

—Oh!

He turned.

—What?

—Nothing.

—I won't be a minute. Finish your coffee.

In his room he threw the paper on the bed and gathered together his paints and rags and brushes. He took the canvas without looking at it.

—People who tell pretty lies only do it because they can't accept the beautifulness of truth.

Miranda had said that.

Graham had said:

—It's "beauty," not "beautifulness," and stop trying to be philosophical.

All the same he took the canvas without looking at it, knowing that it was a lie, knowing that he would sell it for two or three hundred pounds and that a critic, somewhere, would say that Graham Winter was undoubtedly a painter of considerable charm.

When he got downstairs the girl was waiting for him.

They went together and sat by the plate-glass window and Graham said:

—Don't bother to pose today. Just sit any old how.

He had not intended saying this but, the words being spoken, he did not retract them. Having unintentionally challenged his own dishonesty, he was too honest to ignore the challenge.

In any case, to begin with it made no difference. The girl sat still as usual, her golden eyes reflecting nothing from a point over his right shoulder, her face poised between tension and oblivion. After a while, though, she spoke.

—Do you mind if I talk? she said.

—No. That's what I meant. Just . . . be natural.

—How long will you be staying?

—Here? asked Graham, painting brown shadows at the base of her neck.

—Yes.

—Oh, I don't know. They'll be shutting up the hotel soon.

—Then what will you do?

He looked at her. She was watching him. Her eyebrows were drawn together in expectation of his answer and he noticed how thick they were.

—Blast, he thought. I've done them all wrong.

Dipping his brush into mounds of brown and yellow paint, he began to rectify the eyebrows on the canvas.

—I'll stay as long as I can, he said, then back to England. I've got a studio in Kensington.

—That's odd, said the girl. I somehow imagined you living all alone in a cottage in Cornwall, say, or Scotland. A sort of wild eccentric, roaming the moors with your canvases and easel, terrifying the local peasants. Artists and Kensington. They don't seem to go together.

He could hear that she was smiling. He looked up at her again and saw that he was right. Her mouth had curled down at the corners, folding her skin into dimples.

—That's how she smiles, he thought. In a way that isn't asking for anything. Women normally want something when they smile at you.

He wiped his brush on a rag wet with turpentine, dried it across the fabric of his jeans and covered it with new colors to try and capture the smile. But the smile had gone and the girl was saying:

—I'm not moving too much, am I?

—No, said Graham.

But she was. Far too much.

As she spoke of this and that, and Graham did not hear the words she used, his brush raced across the canvas, from canvas to paint, in a new fury, creating impressions before Graham had time to analyze them, molding moods and expressions and thoughts that were feelings and feelings so fleeting that thoughts could not hold them and finally showing what Graham had known and had dreamed of in dreams he'd forgotten and . . .

The girl was saying:

—. . . friend of mine who ended up having to work in a factory sweeping the floors just because nobody . . .

And:

—Shut up! said Graham.

Thrick, thrick, thrick went the crickets on the flagstones. In the kitchen lunch was being prepared. The sound of china plates. The smell of vegetables and steam. The murmur of French voices talking of other things.

—I'm so sorry, said Graham. I can't imagine what . . .

He had been painting the girl's hands when he had realized, finally, that she was a man.

7

The shock did not awaken into thought until he had reached his bedroom and when it did the only word that came to him was:

—Why?

He did not doubt the certainty of his discovery, having always half known it, having seen it in the wrists that were strong enough to support the weight of a body hanging, having seen it, even before that, in legs that were too straight and hard for the stockings they wore, in a face that should have been a boy's. But . . .

—Why? he said aloud.

—Why on earth should anyone . . . ? No wonder we none of us guessed. The whole thing's so unlikely, so stupid.

And yet he could not justify the dread he felt nor the fact that he had not confronted the girl . . . boy . . . with his knowledge.

He went to the window and leaned out. The blistered

shutters, hooked back, nagged at their fastenings. Sea gulls circled low over the earth and behind them the sky rolled like smoke.

—More rain, he thought. Then:

—Why didn't I just say to her: "I know all about you"? Why didn't I just ask her? Why?

—Perhaps . . . , he thought. Perhaps . . .

He crushed his head between the tips of his fingers. He tried to reason but logic was incapable of resolving such apparent illogicality.

—Perhaps he's just a pervert who . . . Perhaps he's trying to hide from . . .

Arguments formed and crumbled in his brain. Solutions suggested themselves and were dismissed. Only the bewilderment, the question mark, the sudden feeling of having been dragged out of his depth were real. He could accept these but not the beginnings of answers whose ends were too grotesque to imagine.

He turned from the window. Glass slammed behind him.

Looking for some ordinary thing to do, he saw the folded copy of the *Times* that he had thrown on the bed hours ago. The neatly folded copy of yesterday's newspaper.

—She can't have had time to read it yet, he thought.

He stopped.

He went to the bed.

He sat down on the bed.

With a gesture that was mechanical he laid the paper flat and began to turn the pages. The back page: the crossword, the announcements of birth and death; the business news; the sports news.

He turned them slowly, trying to see what it could be in the English papers that had been disturbing her. The room, now with the window closed, was very quiet. He did not know what he was looking for, only that when he saw it he would recognize it.

The arts page; the women's page. He was hardly reading the blurred print, merely turning, turning, as in a ritual which had been known to yield miracles.

The overseas news; the home news. Then there it was.

He had almost passed it by the time it registered in the conscious part of his mind. So improbable. So inevitable. A smudged photograph of a boy who was Judy without makeup, with short hair, and beside it the photograph of a woman he did not know and below that an article.

ACTRESS FOUND DEAD IN MORTLAKE FLAT

MONDAY, SEPT. 19—Twenty-five-year-old actress Miss Judy Keeble, Sir John's secretary in the popular television series "Dog Eat Dog," was yesterday evening found dead in the bedroom of her two-roomed flat in Mortlake. A police spokesman said that she had died from head injuries, probably caused by a blunt instrument.

Miss Keeble's body was discovered by the landlord, Mr. Thomas Atkin of Barnes, when he came to collect the rent. He rang the doorbell and receiving no answer let himself into the flat with his own key. He discovered the actress's body lying fully clothed on the bedroom floor.

The police say that she had been dead for some time.

They are making inquiries into the whereabouts of the late woman's husband, actor Robin Howard.

Graham Winter, artist, in a room in a hotel in a fishing village on the Atlantic coast of France, folded his copy of the London *Times* and stood up. It was half-past two in the afternoon.

He went to the mahogany wardrobe by the window of his room and took from it a crew-necked cashmere sweater, bought from Lillywhite's in Piccadilly Circus by his one-time mistress, Miranda, and pulled it over his head. He combed his hair, not gray but the color of old twine, so that it flicked up above his ears and over the frayed collar of his cotton shirt. He saw that his face was calm.

Taking in one hand the newspaper that he had been reading, he left his room, closing the door behind him. The landing smelled of polish and sand. On the walls there were English hunting prints.

He went down stone stairs into the lounge of the hotel.

There, at one of the tables, a young man in a woman's beige linen suit sat playing patience. At the sound of Graham Winter's footsteps the young man looked up and said, in a voice that was soft and did not belie his female apparel:

—Are you going out?

—For a walk, said Graham Winter.

—Can I come with you?

—Yes. Of course.

—You don't mind, do you? You weren't going to work or . . . ?

—No. No, I'd like you to come with me.

They left the hotel together. The glass doors slammed behind them, swinging once, twice, before coming to rest.

The road they took was empty, for it was early in the afternoon. Their feet slapped against the tarmac as they walked. The older man wore sneakers, the younger a pair of crocodile-skin shoes with lowish heels. He wore them easily as though through habit or practice. He was saying:

— . . . rang up the station for me and she says there's a train that leaves Quimper at ten forty-five which'll get me into Paris sometime tomorrow morning.

—I see, his companion said. He walked with his lips parted, his nostrils drawn, for he was not a young man and they were going fast.

At a bend in the road they turned to the left, over rocks and onto the peninsula that the villagers called the Fin du Monde. The men moved more slowly now and neither of them spoke. The air was possessed by the birds and the wind.

To the right of them, some distance off, a lighthouse blinked and ahead of them a steamer like a cardboard cut-out followed the gray line of the horizon.

At the edge of the world the artist stopped and the young man stopped too, a few feet behind him. The artist shifted in his hand the newspaper that he had taken from his room. He said, not looking at the younger man and quietly:

—There's something here I think might interest you.

He passed the paper back and said:

—Page two.

Before him the rocks fell down five hundred feet. Pebbles dislodged themselves and fluttered like paper to the sea. It was an unsafe place to stand.

He took from the pocket of his jeans some cigarettes and a lighter. He bent his head, nurturing the flame between his hands and chest until the loose ends of tobacco caught fire. He exhaled the smoke from his lungs. It whipped away from him like cotton.

———

Graham stood at the cliff edge and waited: for the rustle of tiny stones, for the sudden hand to push him. He heard the page of the newspaper turn. He heard the silence that followed. His feet gripped the rocks through the rubber soles of his shoes, his knees were flexed, his back was braced. He thought:

—Any minute now. Any minute now he'll know that I've found him out.

Sweat needled his armpits. The cigarette between his lips was dry. At school there had been a game that they had played in a darkened room in which one of the boys would hide behind a curtain or in a closet ready to jump out and catch you at the least expected moment. How they had strained their ears to catch the telltale sound of creaking boards, to chart the whisper of their fellows' halted breathing.

Graham had enjoyed the game. He enjoyed it now. If his throat tightened, if his stomach melted at the thought of the brave thing he was doing, some other part of him knew equally well that this murderer was only Judy after all and that men like himself do not die or suffer calamities. They stand at the brink of other people's disasters.

He thought:

—Behind me a man is standing who has killed his wife and may now try to kill me. I'm taking a great risk, coming alone with him to this place. If I should feel his hand between my shoulder blades . . .

But he knew that this would not happen, because he could not imagine it. And when it did not, then he would also know that the . . . the man was not really a cold-blooded killer, just . . .

He could not, at that moment, think of another name by which to call someone who has battered his wife to death.

He thought:

—Judy Keeble was two evenings ago found dead. She died from head injuries caused by a blunt instrument. The police are making inquiries into the whereabouts of the late woman's husband, actor Robin Howard.

Looking down he saw the ocean with her scarcely concealed rockheads.

He thought:

—He's only a child, for God's sake, not a . . . I'll help him. It's my duty to help him. He won't push me. He'll cry and ask me not to betray him and I shall say that there is no need for him to explain. I understand.

Robin Howard dropped the newspaper. It fell to the ground with a beating of ungainly wings. He said:

—I suppose that's that then.

Graham heard him speak and turned to face him. Seeing Judy standing there he could say nothing. He had expected . . . not a murderer, no, but at least a boy, the boy in the smudged photograph.

—Well, said Robin Howard. Now you know.

—Yes, said Graham.

He thought:

—Why hasn't she changed?

—How long have you known? asked Robin.

—Not long, said Graham.

And yet, still he did not know. It was like one of those terrible pictures of lines that do not meet and yet appear to. A puzzle for children. What is and isn't?

Robin said:

—I'm sorry. It must have been quite a shock, learning everything like that.

—Yes, said Graham.

He thought:

—I am talking to a man who has murdered his wife.

But Judy was still standing there, so he said:

—Well, what do we do now?

The newspaper was restless between them on the ground. Robin Howard bent to pick it up. His hair fell over his face, thick like candle wax. His nose was too big for a girl. He gathered the pages of the paper together then folded it into eight and stood up.

—Here, he said.

—Thanks, said Graham, taking the paper from Judy with her thick white hair, her too large nose.

—Shall we go then? said Robin.

—Where?

—To the police, I suppose.

Graham remembered reading that a man was wanted for having brutally murdered his wife, remembered thinking that a young boy was in trouble and needed his help. He said:

—Why did you do it?

It did not seem like an important question.

Above them clouds were drawn like fingers and like elephants.

Robin Howard turned from Graham Winter. He looked to the harbor, where the ferry moved with silent chains laboring the water, and he said:

—I don't know.

He said:

—We'd only been married eight months. We were married in January. It was freezing cold and she wore a white coat. There was a man from the press there and lots of her friends. Actors mainly. People from the series she was in. And my parents.

—I don't think anyone quite believed it was actually happening. Mum and Dad certainly didn't. Nor did her friends for that matter. They thought she was mad. She was much older than me, you see, seven years older, and . . . and quite successful. She was in this television series. Well, you read that. And I was just a drama student who'd been kicked out of college after his first year. I'd met her through a friend of a friend and . . . Oh, in any case, it was terribly cold and she was looking beautiful and I was drunk and . . .

—You see, what had happened was . . . what she had said was: "If you want to make an honest woman of me, then that's your lookout. I don't mind. It might be quite fun and at least I know you'll be faithful."

He paused. He tilted his head to the sky so that tears should not fall and bewilder him. After a while he continued.

—In any case, he said, that's not the point. The point is this: Murder is a very easy thing to do.

He was facing Graham now.

—You just take someone by the shoulders and you smash them, you smash their head against a radiator. You do it once, you do it twice, you do it three, four, five times. And you mustn't listen to them, you mustn't take any notice of what they're saying. You must just *do* it, as many times as you have to until they . . . until they don't *move* anymore. Until they're as . . . still . . . as that.

Then for a while he said nothing, looking only at the hand that he held motionless before his face. Neither did Graham speak.

Later the boy's hand dropped to his side and he said:

—Graham, I didn't mean to kill her.

But Graham did not hear him. Graham had not been listening to him. Graham was a spectator, after all, free to let his mind wander, and in his mind an idea was stirring, so incredible and yet so simple that he was transfixed by it.

—But of course! he thought. But of course! Why on earth didn't I see it before? The answer to every riddle that was ever set is staring us right in the face and we none of us see it.

58

—"When is a door not a door?" Why, when it's ajar, of course. And children understand this because they know that words mean nothing. If a word can mean two things then it means nothing at all. A table, for instance. A table is a table while we call it that. But what if we chose to call it a pirate's ship? Or a space rocket? What if we should lie on it and go to sleep? Isn't it then a bed? And Daddy is sometimes "Mr. Brown" and sometimes "darling," isn't he? And "darling" can be angry or reproachful or forgiving, can't it?

—The nature of an object is entirely dependent on the name by which you choose to call it—nothing else. It's the words, thought Graham, the words. That's it. That's the answer. If you want to understand, then you've got to forget the words. No—not forget them. Not forget them but learn, somehow, to cope with them.

He was staring now at the boy who was wearing a woman's suit, at the girl who had once been a man.

—Somehow, he thought. To cope with the words somehow. Somehow.

—Graham? said Robin.

—Yes, said Graham.

There were elephants and fingers in the sky above him.

—Graham? Have you been listening? Did you hear what I said?

—Yes, said Graham.

Then, carefully:

—Yes, Judy.

8

Madame Bonnet had a cousin in the village who ran a car-hire firm. That is to say owned a secondhand Peugeot in which the locals, in exchange for small considerations, made their infrequent trips to town and from which, at rather more expense, the tourists could inspect the natural beauties of the headland.

This cousin's name was Alphonse Peneau and at three thirty-five on the afternoon of Tuesday the twentieth of September Graham went to see him.

As he opened the wooden gate that led into Peneau's yard a bell rang out above his head and lean gray dogs like whippets barked, straining at their chains. He looked around him. There were cartons with empty wine bottles and the rusted mudguard of a tractor, windfall apples and a carpenter's trestle table, an empty rabbit hutch, a rain barrel, some sheets of corrugated iron. On the doorstep a girl with dark eyes sat and watched him.

—Hello, said Graham in French. Your father, is he at home?

The girl stood up and left him. From the shadow of the doorway he heard her call.

—Daddy! There's a gentleman here to see you.

The dogs had stopped barking. They lay on the crooked flagstones and watched him.

A window above Graham's head opened and the shutters were pushed back. A man leaned out.

—What's all the noise? he asked.

—Monsieur Peneau? said Graham.

—That's me.

—My name is Graham Winter. I'm staying at the Hotel . . .

—Ah! said Peneau. The English artist! One minute, please, monsieur.

The head withdrew. The dark-green shutters closed behind it.

—And now, said Peneau when he had reappeared at ground level. What can I do for you, monsieur? You wish, perhaps, to hire my car?

—Yes, said Graham. I'm taking the young English lady to the station this afternoon and I thought I might stay in town for a couple of days. The weather . . .

He indicated the lowering gray skies.

—Ah, yes, said Peneau. Summer dies and the tourists and the swallows leave hastily before the funeral.

He threw back his big black head and laughed. He was a coffinmaker and enjoyed jokes about death.

—In any case, he said, about the car. You have a license?

61

—Yes.

—Good. Good. Then there's no problem, is there? Come, let me show her to you. She's a good car. Old but affectionate. Don't drive her too hard, remember to keep to the right and you'll have no trouble, I can guarantee.

Peneau led Graham round to the side of the house where the Peugeot stood among asters and loosestrife and bedraggled brown hens. He said:

—So the young English lady is going home, is she?

—That's right, said Graham.

The lie came easily.

—Well, now, said Peneau. There's the ignition. Those are the lights, the windscreen wipers, the dimmer. You'll have to watch it a bit in second gear, it sometimes slips, but apart from that . . . She didn't stay here long then, did she?

—Who?

—But the young lady, of course.

—No. No, as a matter of fact she's had to go back sooner than she thought, said Graham. Some trouble at home, I believe. A grandmother died or an aunt or something. They need her there.

The lie came very easily.

—But, sir, said Graham to the headmaster of his preparatory school. But, sir, it's not a real lie. It's only in fun. It's only a game we're playing.

—I see, Winter. It's only a game, is it?

—Oh, no, sir. I didn't mean that. I meant . . . No, sir, this is for real. A lady's life is at stake. I'm lying to protect a lady, sir.

—Are you sure you know quite what you *are* doing, Winter?

Graham ran the back of his hand across his forehead. It was as though Peneau's eyes were the sun and he had grown dizzy from staring too long into them.

—In any case, he said, I've said I'll drive her to the station. I believe there's a train that leaves for Paris sometime tonight. It seemed the best thing to do.

—Oh, quite, said Peneau. Now, about money.

They agreed upon terms. Graham got into the car, which was large with cracked gray leather seats and a pervading smell of linseed oil. He said:

—Well, good-bye then and thank you.

As he drove off down the path he looked in the mirror and saw Peneau by the wooden gate, in overalls and a collarless shirt, with his big red face and his short black hair like the bristles of a brush, counting the notes he had given him.

In the foyer of the hotel Judy waited with suitcases. Madame Bonnet and Giles were also there.

—Ah! said Madame Bonnet. You're all leaving us!

—I'll be back, said Graham.

Then added:

—Not for a couple of days though.

This was an important part of his plan. In two days they would have reached Marseilles. In two days Judy would be on a ship to North Africa. In two days Graham would . . . This part was not yet clear but in two days . . .

—Au revoir, madame, he said. Au revoir, Giles.

—Au revoir, said Judy.

They picked up their suitcases and left the hotel. The enamel tables, the canvas chairs, the faded red-and-green umbrellas that usually stood in front of the hotel had been folded up and were leaning against a wall. The air was wet with autumn. Graham put the cases in the boot of the car.

—Come on, he said. No, the other side. We're in France, remember.

Judy got into the passenger seat. Graham got in beside her. He closed the door and put the key in the ignition.

—That seemed to go off all right, didn't it? he said.

He started the engine. He pressed down the clutch and moved the gear into first. He released the clutch. With a sigh the car began to move.

—Graham, said Judy as they crested the hill and began the short downward run to the harbor. I do appreciate what you're doing, I really do, but all the same . . .

—Shhh, said Graham.

—No one can hear us.

—That's not the point.

—Well, what is then?

When they reached the harbor the ferry was waiting for them. Graham drove the car up the metal-slatted gang-plank, half expecting a man to cry:

—Halt! Who goes there?

Once they were on board, a sailor in a blue sweater with the name of the vessel in red across his chest sold them a ticket.

Leaning against an iron railing, Graham and Judy watched green waves slurp, watched hungry gulls fly low for bread.

—Listen. Just tell me why you're doing it, that's all.

—Because, look, whatever happened—what*ever* happened—I don't think you deserve to be punished.

—But I do! Oh, Graham, I do. That's just it.

—Nonsense.

—You ought to have handed me in.

—Please. Give me credit for some insight into your character. If you were a killer, a real killer, you'd have pushed me off that cliff this afternoon.

—I've deceived you before, haven't I?

Graham did not answer this. He watched the moorings being released, the quay receding.

—In any case, I could have got a train. That way you needn't have become involved.

—I've told you. Don't go on about it.

—I've got a right to know, haven't I?

—Just trust me, Judy, will you?

—I do trust you. It's not that.

—Well, then?

Graham did not like unanswered questions either but he knew, now, that whatever answers were given had to be the right ones. They had to be chosen with care. The words must be the right words. There were rules. So, eventually, he said:

—If you'd gone by train, alone, the chances are that the police would have stopped you. They're not fools, you know. The idea that you'll be in disguise will've occurred to them. But with me, you see, speaking the language, in a French car . . .

When Graham had decided to accompany Judy to Mar-

65

seilles it had not been for this reason. Having formulated the idea, it became the only reason there had ever been.

I suppose you're right, said Judy. Oh, I'm sorry. I know I'm sounding incredibly ungrateful.

—No, you're not.

—I am. I know I am. It's just that, really, I almost wish you had told the police about me. Oh, I know that sounds stupid but . . . It's like when you're being chased, you know, and one half of you wants to run as fast as you can and the other half just wants to stop and get it over with.

—Then you'd better concentrate on the half that wants to run.

—I have been. I have been. But if only you knew how difficult it was. Especially now when you know and I can't pretend to myself that it never happened.

Her voice was rough. It caught in her throat as though she found it hard to articulate what she was thinking.

—I don't know if I can go on, she said.

—I can, said Graham, the tower of strength, the knight on the white horse.

At the other side of the bay they drove the car down a metal-slatted gangplank and onto another road.

—We're off, said Graham.

It was by now twenty to five. On either side of them as they left the sea the land stretched flat and long to the horizon. The sky was the color of dying roses. Cars slipped toward them and dissolved behind them. Cars piled high with holiday luggage, cars with children pressing their noses to the steamy windows, English cars returning to Calais and Le Havre. They overtook some too. Little Deux

66

Chevaux Citroëns bouncing from side to side and lorries carrying yogurt or spare parts for washing machines.

Judy found a radio beneath the dashboard and turned it on. A boy with a guitar sang:

> *Mon amour des vacances.*
> *Demain tu rentres chez toi,*
> *La ville t'engloutira,*
> *Trop vite tu m'oublieras,*
> *Mon amour des vacances.*
> *Baise-moi encore une fois,*
> *Retiens-moi dans tes bras,*
> *Trop vite tu m'oublieras . . .*

The smoke from Graham's cigarette curled round inside the car, forming a canopy beneath the roof. The tires hummed against the road, the odometer turned, the needle on the petrol gauge sank.

At a gray town with a river and a cathedral Graham stopped to refuel. He told the pump attendant that he and his wife were returning to Limoges from their holiday by the sea where, yes, they had enjoyed themselves very much and but what a bad summer it had been, what terrible weather.

Judy sat back in her seat like a shadow, like an echo humming to the radio.

—Is there anywhere round here we can eat? Graham asked the man, standing by him as he checked the oil.

—That depends, monsieur. There is a restaurant, in the square, but I don't know if they'll be serving yet. There are bars, of course: sandwiches, coffee. Was that what you had in mind?

—That'll be fine.

—Then I know a place that'll do you very well, just along the road. Very nice, very clean, very cheap.

—Thanks, said Graham.

They sat at a corner table so that they could talk and ended up saying nothing, watching instead the young men huddled round the pinball machine, the old men playing cards, the three-legged Alsatian that crashed from table to table, the condensation sliding down the blue-enameled, uneven walls. Through the window the sky had turned from pink to brown. There were no stars, no moon.

Back in the car again, Judy said:

—Are we driving through the night then?

—We'll have to.

—But why? We're all right. Nobody knows yet.

—Listen. I shouldn't think there's a police station on the continent that hasn't got your picture by now. They're not slow, those boys, Interpol or whatever they're called. They'll have got the information out in no time at all. It's not as if you're a common shoplifter, or something.

—I do know that.

—Well. I'm sorry.

He was not sorry. He was angry that she could not appreciate the danger they were in, into which he had placed himself. The murder had been discovered two days ago, had been committed a week ago. It was madness to think that the police would not be onto her by now.

Above all it was essential that their flight should not be absurd.

If she was not frightened, then his courage became ridiculous.

—In any case, he said, even if they're not onto you yet there's no point in taking chances, is there? I mean, I daresay you're right and there's certainly no need to panic but still, I'm not tired, I don't need much sleep at the best of times. Besides, it's fun driving at night. No?

—Yes, Graham.

In the darkness she touched his hand.

—I'm sorry.

The adventure was redeemed.

At four o'clock they drove onto the side of the road and slept. Already day was beginning to break. The night was officially over.

9

A car woke him—one of the many that must have passed through their sleep.

And before he had time to open his eyes the morning began its assault upon his senses, filling his stomach with the heavy smells of sleep, of warm leather, of dead cigarettes, making him aware of the mat texture of his mouth, quickening the pain in his right leg where it had been forced against the gear stick, dampening his face, his hair with sunlight.

He opened his eyes and the golden day blinded him.

He closed his eyes and opening them again saw the road like a flung ribbon of shot silk before him, saw, to his left and down, the white stream that paralleled the road, saw to his right a hillside, thick with oaks and beech trees, climbing almost vertically to the sky.

In this place, on this day, the birds flew singly. Not like the swallows. They beat their passage to places beyond the hills with powerful red legs outstretched, their larger shadows trailing the treetops.

70

In the car, beside Graham, the girl slept. Neither had she escaped the morning.

It poured over her, it burst from her, it burst from her head like a young warrior goddess. It caught at her breathing and held it like incense about her lips. She was enchanted.

Everything was enchanted.

A magic current leaped from the sky to the earth, from the earth to the girl, achieving power within Graham.

The car was too small for him then. Edging closer to the door, he leaned upon the handle. It glided away from him. He stepped onto the tarmac and felt the world turn beneath his feet.

From the woods the impatient voices of hood-eyed goshawks came. Purple doves called to him. Boars with cloven hoofs and halberd tusks tore at the savage undergrowth and there were unicorns and there were centaurs—dark hair clung to their legs—who plashed in green rivers and tasted blood between their teeth.

There was something else.

In the heart of the forest, surrounded by a tall stone wall, surrounded by ivy with birds' nests and empty eggshells, surrounded by trees whose incestuously tangled branches blackened the sun, a castle of corridors stood and masked people danced by torchlight through its halls.

Graham, at the edge of the wood, may have known that he was happy.

—Hey! What's happening?

She leaned from the car doorway, her hands gripping the window ledge behind her, her body thrust into the morning. His morning.

—Hello, he said, embarrassed as though she had caught him sleeping.

—What are you doing there?

—Me? Oh, nothing . . . Thinking. Stretching my legs.

They met halfway between the car and the woods.

—Where are we then?

He looked beyond her.

—Well, if I'm right we should be somewhere near a town called Aurillac. In the Auvergne. We're nearly there, Judy.

—Already? she said.

Graham looked at his watch.

—Well . . .

—How much further? About?

—We should be in Marseilles by lunchtime.

She walked away from him. She held her elbows to her as though she were cold. A long way from him she said:

—It's all right here.

He could not see her face. Her suit was creased.

—We'll have to go, he said.

—Yes.

—It's not quite the moment for sightseeing. Hey?

—No. I was just thinking that.

—What?

—You know. What a way to see a country for the first time. Like this.

—You've never been here before, then?

72

—No.

He went to her.

—Come on.

—Couldn't we . . . I don't know . . . bathe or something?

—No.

The river below them on the far side of the road was like cream. Young boys could have slithered down its banks and dipped their poodle heads beneath the water.

—No! Look, Judy. Listen. Let's get this straight. As far as I'm concerned we can do anything you want. We can swim or we can go for a walk or . . . we can have a picnic even. I don't care. I'm not doing this for myself, you know. And what's more . . .

The grass was brittle beneath his feet.

—And what's more, I'm not forcing you to do anything you don't want to do. It's entirely your decision. It's a wonderful morning. If you want to stay here we'll stay here. Only . . .

—Graham!

—No, listen.

—I'm listening. I am listening. What are you getting so het up about?

—I'm not getting het up.

—You are. I mean, please, I'm not trying to be difficult but . . . Graham, just . . . why don't you just leave me here? Go back to the hotel. Go back to your holiday. Let me make my own way out of this.

—I never said that.

—I know you didn't. Just . . . Please.

She held her hands in a gesture of prayer, except that her

fists were clenched. Graham made himself weaker than she.

—I'm asking you to let me help you, he said.

—Let me, Judy.

She moved backward from him. The heels of her croco-dile-skin shoes brushed the dry grass. She turned her face from him.

—All right, she said. Race me.

She spun away from him and ran toward the car. Graham followed her. He looked to the horizon for black clouds but the sky was empty. Holiday blue. Neither were there any police cars with flashing lights when he checked in the rear-view mirror before driving away from that place.

—Look! "Avignon—twenty kilometers"! she said.

—We'll eat there. We'll have to eat soon. You can get washed and tidied up too.

Graham had looked at the girl and seen that she was tired and hungry. He assumed that that was why she was behaving so carelessly.

Her face was pale and her makeup had slipped into gray lines and creases. Her skin had a kind of uneasy roughness about the chin, a kind of . . . He repeated:

—You can get washed and . . . well, you know.

The girl said:

—Avignon. That's the place with the bridge, isn't it?

—Only half of one now, said Graham.

—Really? What happened to the other bit? Too much dancing?

74

Graham's eyes flashed up to the driving mirror again. They were alone on the road. He wondered whether that was not unusual.

—It probably just crumbled away, he said. It's very old. This is a pretty old part of France. D'you know, there are volcanoes up in some of those hills.

The girl was silent for a while. She wound down the window and leaned her head out of it. The wind of their passage whipped her hair like blows across her face. Then:

—Eighteen kilometers, she said.

—What?

She came back into the shell of the car.

—Eighteen kilometers. How far does that make it to Marseilles?

—An hour. Or two.

Then she said:

—Africa.

—What?

—Africa. Algeria. It doesn't . . . I mean, somehow it doesn't seem real, does it? Can you believe it?

Graham pressed his foot hard against the accelerator. It sank beneath his weight and the noise of the engine rose correspondingly high, drowning the girl's words. He pulled down the steering wheel to round a bend.

—Jesus Christ! Why doesn't that silly bastard look where he's going?

The man with the horse and cart stood up on his box and waved after them in a pathetic dumb show of fury.

—We could have had an accident, said Graham.

Graham came to a decision.

He felt in the glove box for the packet of cigarettes and put one in his mouth. Bracing his legs against the driving seat and steering with one hand, he took the lighter from his back pocket and flicked open the lid. A small blue flame quivered, caught the loose ends of tobacco and died. He threw the lighter onto the ledge in front of him.

—Judy.

—Yes?

—I want to ask you something. Only I don't want you to feel that you've got to answer, he said.

—O.K.

—It's . . . Well, I don't want so much to "ask you" as . . . Look, would you rather not talk about it?

—Oh, she said. I see.

—What?

—What do you want to know?

—Nothing. Just . . .

—Why I killed her? I suppose you've got a right to know.

Graham flicked a nervous pile of ash onto the floor of the car.

—No. I know that. You've told me that.

—Not really.

—Well . . . Yes, you have.

—I don't know why I did it. You'd probably be able to think up a better reason than I could. It just happened, that's all. I mean, if you want to put it into words . . .

76

—Yes.

—Well, I suppose I was jealous. I lost my temper and . . . Oh!

—Had she been unfaithful to you?

Graham spoke softly now. He made his voice soft. The engine purr was like an anesthetic to his words.

—That? said the girl, as if she had not quite heard him, winding the window up so that the car was still.

—That? Oh, yes. Oh, yes, oh, yes. It was that sort of . . . marriage. God, I even shared her on our wedding night. With some producer in television. I had her till eight, then off she went to him. Just like that. It was my fault. I knew what I'd let myself in for. She hadn't tried to hide it from me. She always said that one day I'd grow up and realize what she was about.

—But . . . why?

—The thing is, though, you can't take it forever. You keep hoping, you see, and then one day you find you haven't got any strength left to hope with. You can't go on forever pretending and pretending that everything's all right. You can't go on accepting something that's hurting you like that. Every day some new pain, just when you're least expecting it. Not regularly, because there were times when we were happy together. But then you were that much weaker, that much less resistant. And then one day you find you just can't take it anymore.

—I suppose that's what happened, she said. Do you think you understand now?

—Of course, said Graham.

77

—Of course you don't. Oh, well, it doesn't matter. What did you want to know then, if it wasn't that?

—I do understand. But . . . the rest? Afterward, I mean. What did you do then?

—Afterward?

—Yes, said Graham.

He leaned forward to wipe a mark from the windscreen.

—What do you mean? said the girl.

Graham meant that he wanted to know the whole story. It was a story, after all. It had a beginning and an end. He knew those. But what had happened in between? He had to get it right if he was to play his part. The guest star in a popular serial. He said:

—I'm trying to understand you.

He leaned back in his seat. The windscreen was clear.

—Well, next, I suppose . . . I can't remember. I knew I had to get out and . . . That's right. I know. I was quite calm about the whole thing.

She laughed then.

—God knows how, but I was. Almost as if someone else was doing the thinking for me. I don't know, some angel or some . . . what is it? Instinct of self-preservation? Oh, it's so difficult to explain. I mean, after what I'd . . . what I'd done. But my head seemed, you know, incredibly clear and . . . just thoughts and plans. No feelings. I mean, I wasn't panicking at all. I just worked out that I had to get away. I had to go somewhere and start again. I mean . . .

—Yes?

—Well, it was almost as if I suddenly *was* someone else. A new person. If I could just get away from that room, from

78

. . . what I'd done, I suppose. I mean everything. The whole muck-up. Being an actor, being married to her, being a failure. My whole life.

—But what did you *do*?

Graham kept his eyes on the road. He had not wanted this: reasons, explanations. Just facts.

—What did you *do*? he said.

—I worked out a plan. I got a suitcase down from the cupboard and then . . . and then I got her passport and her money and her clothes and makeup and I packed them. Then I took a taxi to the airport and got the first plane I could to Paris. All this on my passport, you see.

—Paris?

—Yes. I don't know. France was the nearest country, I suppose.

—What were you going to do there?

—Nothing. Well, I mean, just start again. Just . . . I chucked my passport into a rubbish bin at . . . what's it called? Orly. It was like a gesture.

—And?

—Well, you can see. I went into a gents' loo, still at the airport, into a cubicle and got changed into her clothes. She was the same size as me, just about. I used to . . .

She hesitated.

—I used to wear her things sometimes. She liked it. Oh! Not like that. She . . . thought it was funny, I suppose. She always said I could have been a girl. She used to make me up too. Well, you know, for fun.

—God! said Graham.

There was a sickness in his throat.

—No. I mean, it wasn't . . . It was just a joke.

Graham changed gear, needing the feeling of power this action gave him, needing all the power he could muster to overcome the nausea that threatened him, to concentrate on the future of which he was in control rather than on this horrible, this incomprehensible past. He said:

—So after that you just walked out?

—Well, I waited, of course, until I couldn't hear anyone. Then I went and found a shoeshop.

—A shoeshop?

—I had to. Hers were killing me. I thought: "If they guess in here that I'm not a woman then I'll know it's all up." I didn't mind. But they didn't. So I really thought, I really believed I'd done it. Then I went into one of those booths where you get your photograph taken and I put the picture of me into her passport. It was so easy. The Bonnets never noticed, at the hotel, did they?

—God, yes. We're going to have to watch out for that when . . .

—It'll be all right.

—I'll work something out, said Graham, changing back into top gear.

—In any case, that's it. I got the train to Quimper and arrived at Benmel on Thursday night. I'd seen it on a map and I'd thought . . . you know . . . it was so small and remote and there wouldn't be anyone there really and I'd be able to find a job or something. Well, that's what I'd thought and . . . Oh, well . . .

They drove in silence over the wide Rhône into Avignon.

10

Another hotel.

In the Place de l'Horloge, at a round check-clothed table made secret by potted greenery, they ate bouillabaisse, lamb and blue cheese. The meal was a cleansing and a feeding. In the sediment of the wine, in the grounds of the coffee, the morning was dissolved.

Graham was pleased that it should be so. It had been necessary to establish certain situations, to explain certain mysteries. It had been necessary but now it had to be forgotten.

—*This* is where we really begin, he thought.

In a town that is not your home you may go for absolution. There are churches and there are restaurants.

—Judy, some more coffee?
—No, thank you.

The collar of her suit was turned up at one side. Not at the back, as though she had intended it to be so. She ran her finger round the rim of a glass, making it squeak.

—Well, said Graham.

He leaned toward her. He leveled his body with his elbows.

—About your passport, he said.

—Yes?

—We're going to have to think about that. The photograph not being stamped.

—Yes. I suppose so. It was all right at the hotel though.

—That's not quite the same thing.

—I showed it there. You have to. You know, for the forms and things.

—Yes, he said.

He took the glass from her hand.

—That was different. They have to fill in those forms. It's part of the law. But at the customs in Marseilles, you see . . . Look, Judy, don't you worry. I'll fix something. I should be able to mock something up. Hey?

—Yes, Graham.

She traced the outline of a red square on the tablecloth. She looked at him.

—Thank you, she said.

—No, please.

But he was glad.

From Avignon to Aix-en-Provence, from Aix to Marseilles.

A colorless sun burned to the right of them. Houses with tiled roofs blistered the hillsides. The air was choked with gorse flowers and oranges and lavender, was blue with the haze of olive leaves. Driving with his forearm on the window ledge, Graham watched his skin become the color of apricots. His shirt sleeve, unbuttoned, billowed and flapped. The silver bracelet of his watch caught light.

Every minute, every mile, took them further away.

They reached Marseilles at three o'clock.

—Is this it then? said Judy.

By the labyrinthine, crane-towered complex of the Port Moderne Graham turned the car into a side street and stopped. The engine juddered for a moment, too hot. Down the road some women were arguing. There was no one else.

Graham stretched his legs and felt his flesh rip as it separated from the damp leather.

—Yes, we're here, he said. Now, what next?

It was not a question. More a punctuation. Another chapter heading.

He lit a cigarette and watched the smoke wreathes climb the windscreen.

—The first thing to do is to get your ticket. There's probably some sort of central tourist agency in town where we can do that. Then . . . Well, "then" rather depends on what time your boat sails. In any case, this time tomorrow you should be well on your way.

The women who had been arguing down the road passed

them on the pavement. They had black hair and smelled of fish. When they had gone Judy said:

—I still can't believe it.

—What?

—Any of this. It's been so sudden. One minute . . .

She began to run her fingers through her hair then stopped, as though the action had tired her.

—I don't know.

—We had to be quick, said Graham.

—I know.

—You do understand?

—Of course.

—Well, then? Come on. Let's go.

He threw away the half-smoked cigarette. No breeze moved it across the cobbles.

—What'll I do there, Graham?

—Where?

At the top of the road he had slowed down to read a street indicator.

—There. You know.

—Africa? Ah, I see. "Centre Ville." We'll head for that and then we can ask. Honestly, there's nothing to worry about. You make it sound like the Congo or something. It's only Algeria. They're quite civilized there. Thriving tourist industry for a start. There'll be thousands of young people. White people. Hippies and things. You'll be able to lose yourself amongst them. And you'll have some money. I've told you.

He had planned it all. He had thought of everything. He could not understand why she was still worried.

84

—Yes, she said. I know. I . . .

—Well, we won't go into all that again. Look, what does that sign say?

—I can't see . . .

—Yes. This looks better. Lots of hotels. There's bound to be something round here.

He leaned from the window and called:

—*Excusez-moi, monsieur. Y a-t-il une agence touristique par ici?*

—*Pardon?*

The old man came to them and peered into the car.

—*Une agence touristique. Pour acheter des billets pour le bateau.*

—Ah! said the old man.

He unbent at the knees and stared down the street, rubbing his chin. After a while his head returned inside the car and said:

—*Quelle sorte de bateau?*

—Oh, really!

—What did he say?

—He wants to know what *kind* of a boat. What does it matter . . . Never mind. Let's try again.

He said:

—*Un bateau pour aller en Algérie, monsieur.*

—*Ah, ça,* said the old man. *Eh bien . . .*

He scratched the back of his neck. He was looking at Judy.

—*Eh bien?* said Graham.

His hands were wet on the steering wheel. A car behind them was hooting and a policeman might appear at any minute. Some children, too, had gathered alongside them, children with wide, gap-toothed mouths. They ran their hands over the body of the car. They pressed upon the car like hyenas.

—Come on, said Graham. We'll find it by ourselves.

He rolled up the window. He leaned his foot upon the accelerator. In a skirmish of exhaust smoke they began to move again.

It was late when they found the booking office. They took their place in a queue. There were people around them with traveler's check and dysentery, with sunburn and complaints about the sanitation in hotels. Judy sat on a padded plastic bench.

—Good afternoon, said Graham when he reached the desk. I should like to book a passage to . . .

He paused. The man behind the desk had bags of water beneath his eyes. He was chewing a pencil, looking beyond Graham at a map of southeast France on the far wall.

—North Africa, said Graham. Algiers?

—Algiers? said the man.

—Yes. Or . . .

—Where, exactly?

—Algiers.

The man took a wad of paper from a shelf beneath the desk. He licked his thumb and flicked through the wad, extracting various sheets and laying them in a pile in front of him. Patches of yellow sweat crept like fog from the shadow of his armpits.

—Saturday, he said.

—Saturday. That's . . . There isn't anything before then?

—Booked up.

—I see. Well . . .

86

—Oran, said the man. There's a boat for Oran tomorrow night.

—Where? I mean, where's that?

—Algeria, said the man.

The people in the queue behind Graham became restless. They shuffled and leaned against the counter.

—I'll have a ticket for Oran then, said Graham.

He took some money from his pocket.

—One?

—Yes, one. Er, where does it go from? What time?

—It's on the ticket. This ship.

The man pointed a gray finger to the improbable name.

—Thank you, said Graham.

He took the ticket and slid it into his wallet. He looked round the hall. There were men in uniforms: couriers, sailors, but no policemen. He looked at Judy. She saw him. He went to the door and out onto the street.

—I've managed to fix you up with a passage for tomorrow night, he said.

They walked along the quay to the place where they had left the car. Lorries and vans passed them. Tied to rusted rings in the wall of the dock, liners and tugs and rowboats fretted in a water that was not the sea, their flanks nudged by drift and oil. Warehouses spewed their contents onto the wharf: wool and leather, wheat and olives, meat and wine. And above them always the cranes swung their necks in arcs across the sky.

The people had emerged too, now that the sun was dying.

Sailors in striped sweaters and blue peaked caps ran up

and down gangplanks or called to each other, leaning on the railings of the ships. There were Arabs in dirty robes and tourists with haversacks and port officials whose sun-roughened necks bulged over the tight white collars of their shirts.

—There wasn't anything earlier, said Graham. Nothing. But we'll be O.K. We'll find a small hotel somewhere in a back street and lie low there until it's time to go. I've got your ticket.

He patted his trouser leg.

—I'll give it to you tomorrow, with the money.

In a street off the Boulevard Vauban they found a hotel. Graham said that he was Judy's uncle and the proprietress did not bother to look amused. She shuffled upstairs with them to their room, showed them the basin, the towels, accepted payment in advance and left them.

—We'll be all right here, said Graham.

He went to the window and pulled the shutters open. The road was a residential one and, apart from a few parked cars, empty.

—Yes. We're all right.

He closed the shutters. The light broke into stripes. He went to the basin and turned on the tap.

—I'm going to wash and shave, he said. I expect you'd like to . . .

He paused.

—Look, he said. I'll just go and find the loo. You do whatever you want now. I'll be a few minutes.

He left the room and set off down the corridor, which smelled of damp plaster. His heart was racing as though he had just escaped an accident.

88

In bed they wore their clothes.

Graham did not sleep. He watched the passing head-lights run across the ceiling. He heard voices in the street and in other rooms. He felt the body beside him that turned and settled, turned and settled like the sea.

He thought once:

—God, if you do exist [this was how he addressed his deity], please make everything all right. For her.

He also thought:

—Well, Miranda, what have you got to say now? At last I've done something definite, I've committed myself, haven't I? I might even end up in prison as a result of it. Would you come and visit me then? Would you be proud of me? Would you tell that man you married: "He was my lover once"?

—No. I don't suppose you would. You'd find some fault. I know you.

—But what? What have I done wrong this time? My motives? I haven't any. I'm not involved with her, with . . . No. Nothing. Or is that what's bothering you? Do you think I ought to be . . . ?

The girl was asleep. Her back was turned to him. She held the pillow in her arms. Where the street light touched her face he could see small white hairs across her cheeks and nose.

—No, Miranda. She's . . .

Graham took his hand from under the sheet and moved it across the pillow until it rested an inch away from the

89

girl's head. He lowered his fingers and they touched her hair. He could smell her hair. It smelled of oil and dust and cigarettes. Taking the weight of his body on one arm, he moved closer to her. He could feel her now. The linen of her suit, the nylon of her stockings.

—Don't wake, he said.

He was shaking. His stomach pounded and his back ached.

—Judy.

The name. Never forget a girl's name.

He could taste her hair. He did not move his mouth.

Outside somebody said:

—*Eh bien, bonsoir, mon cher. A demain.*

Footsteps separated on the cobbles. The starting pedal of a motorbike was kicked. An engine throbbed and stalled.

His mouth ached.

The pedal went down again.

His chest.

The engine hesitated.

His lungs.

The engine hesitated.

His brain.

The engine . . . The engine caught fire.

There was a roar, there was a shout of voices, wheels screeched, rubber burned and the bike dissolved like warmth into the night.

11

In the hotel room there was a mirror and in the mirror, through the half-light of early morning, between dust and the condensation of his own breathing, Graham Winter watched himself.

He was pleased with what he saw, seeing a man who had not slept, whose skin was drawn, whose shirt collar was dirty and turned under at the corners. Seeing a room with bulging wallpaper. Seeing a plastic inverted-tulip lamp-shade and a twisting cord. Seeing a girl with the sheets pulled up around her shoulders lying alone in the dip of a double bed.

The mirror was above a washbasin and Graham held the washbasin in his hands while it pressed into his stomach.

Later he got back into the bed and intended to keep vigil, instead of which he slept.

He was angry at ten o'clock to find the girl up before him.

Angry at having forfeited his possession of the day. Angry at his vulnerability. Angry—and frightened also in his half-awakening—seeing astride the windowsill a boy with long, unstockinged legs, hard legs that reached to the floor and did not belong to the skirt they wore.

—Judy!

Why did she turn so slowly? He needed to see her face.

—Hi!

Her voice. Her face. *Her* voice and face. He concentrated on these.

—Come down from there, he said.

—What for? I'm not going to fall.

—I . . . Come down. You're . . . Anyone can see you there.

She looked at him with eyes like golden mirrors.

—O.K., she said.

Resting her hands on the window ledge, she took the weight of her body, swung it round and lowered it into the room. The skirt fell to her knees.

—All right? she asked.

—Yes, said Graham. Yes. That's better.

—It's nice out there.

Graham pulled his elbows back and sat up in the bed. There was a thickness on his chest. He coughed and the phlegm moved inside him.

—Is it? he said.

—Yes.

—Good.

He thought:

—I'm fifty.

He thought:

—Other men of fifty are being brought breakfast in bed by their wives. They are traveling by train to the office, sitting in the seat they always occupy, anticipating the cup of coffee that their secretary will bring them, the gold-plated carriage clock with which the firm will present them in a few years' time.

—Not me. Not me, Miranda.

—Even if I die tomorrow I shall know that I have driven through France in late September with a girl whose life I have saved and that I have lain beside her in a bed with sheets smelling of dry soap powder. That's not bad, Miranda. Is it?

And he said:

—Sleep all right?

—Fine. Like a log.

—Good. I'm glad. There's no point worrying, is there?

—Oh.

She moved toward the window again.

—No. I'm pretty hungry, she said.

—I expect you are. So am I, for that matter.

He pulled back the sheets and turned so that his feet touched the floor. The linoleum was warm and damp, swelling in bubbles as the paper did from the walls. He reached for his shoes.

—I'll tell you what I'll do then, he said. I don't think you'd better go out so I'll just pop down the road and buy us some food. Stuff we can eat here. You know: bread and things. I won't be long. You'll be O.K., won't you?

—Yes.

—Fine then.

He tied his shoelaces slowly, not wanting to leave her, frightened of what she might become while he was away.

She stood beside the bed now, watching him. Her hair was white in the sun and he noticed with relief that she wore her makeup.

—You won't open the door to anyone, will you? he said.

—I'll be all right.

—I know. Just . . . O.K., I fuss too much.

—No, you don't.

—I'm sure that's what you think.

—I don't.

—It's all right, Judy. I don't mind.

He smiled.

—Come on, he said.

She smiled and when he had left the room she stopped smiling and closed her eyes but Graham did not see this.

Graham went down the ill-lit stairs of the hotel to the lobby, where, crouched in the gloom behind her desk, the proprietress waited.

—Good morning, madame, he said to her in French.

—You're leaving? she said.

—Oh, no. Not yet. I'm going out. I'm just taking a walk. It's a beautiful morning, isn't it?

—If you're not out of your room by twelve I'll have to charge you for another day.

—I see.

Graham felt into his pocket for some notes. He gave them to the woman. On the doorstep a cat was sunning itself.

94

—That'll do, said the hotel proprietress.

—You don't want me to sign anything?

—That'll do.

Graham left. Outside the pavement was warm and his shadow flung itself beyond him, half along the ground, half up the gray brickwork of the buildings. He turned to look at the window of what he supposed to be his room and the glass blinded him with purple and gold.

Then he felt free. He felt like a truant schoolboy. He felt like a dog with spring between his legs.

A short way along the road was a shop called Alimentations but he ignored it, preferring to walk a bit further, telling himself that it looked too expensive or too cheap or something. He wanted to walk. All around him people were working while he was not working and he did not feel guilty. He was in the middle of an adventure about which they knew nothing. The burn of escaping breath at the top of a mountain, the sports master and the other boys half a mile below, the climbing tackle forgotten, the safety net forgotten.

In the end he went into a supermarket with palm trees in the forecourt.

It was cool in there and anonymous enough, untouched by human hand or the threat of conversation. Fans buzzed in high, dark corners and Graham moved behind chromium shelves and the backs of women with metal carts. He chose salami and garlic sausage and prepacked croissants, a bottle of three-franc wine, some grapes in cellophane, a box of cheese. Then he took his place in a queue at one of the check-out desks.

The girls who worked the registers were alike, dark and sweaty. The hair on their upper lip glistened. Their damp red hands reached back and forth, pushing food along, counting money, hitting the keys on the registers. Graham watched them working. He watched the women with bad-tempered faces who shopped. He watched the children too, in transparent plastic sandals and cotton shorts, as they played among the cardboard boxes or pulled at their mothers' skirts.

So it was that he did not notice at first the man who stood behind him in the queue.

He was not, in any case, a man to be noticed, except by virtue of the fact that he was in the supermarket at all.

He was shorter than the average height, five foot five or six, and plump with pale, wispy hair and a large forehead but otherwise unmemorable features. He wore a blue suit and a white shirt. His shoes were black with pointed, well-polished toes. His feet were small.

In the metal basket over his arm he carried a packet of Madeleine biscuits.

Graham saw him as he turned to replace his own basket in the pile beside the desk and noticed him because of the way he was staring at him. Not staring, no. More watching, with small, gray, hooded eyes like the eyes of an owl half-asleep that spreads its wings to become a bird of prey.

The moment Graham had seen him he turned away and began counting out money to pay the outstretched palm in front of him. His own hands were cold like water.

He took his purchases and moved toward the plate-glass door and the palm trees. He opened the door and swung

96

toward himself the reflection of a man not well dressed but carefully dressed, with polished shoes, buying a packet of biscuits.

He began to walk. He crossed the supermarket forecourt. He turned into the street, up the hill, toward the hotel. Once he looked behind him and saw, or thought he saw, a flash of blue serge among the white shirts and brown arms of the Marseillais who thronged the mid morning.

He knew what to do. He had seen it in a hundred films. He took the first turning that he came to and continued walking, turning to left and to right until at last, near the top of the town, he came to a courtyard with an open gate. There he stopped and entered. There was nobody about, only some pigeons and a sea gull strutting across the cobbles.

He moved back into the shadows along one of the tall stone walls that encircled the yard. From the other side of the yard a shuttered house watched him without comment.

He listened.

From a distance he heard the muted clatter of the city, from nearer by the voices of boys.

Hitching the brown paper packet of food beneath his armpit, Graham ran his hands down the sides of his jeans. The rough fabric absorbed his sweat. He thought:

—I must have lost him.

He thought:

—Maybe he wasn't a policeman after all. Perhaps I'm being . . .

A car was pulling up the hill toward him.

—Jesus!

97

—No, thought Graham as the car passed, filling that part of the gateway that he could see from where he stood pressed against the wall with dust.

—No, he was a policeman all right. There's no getting away from that. A man in a supermarket buying a packet of biscuits? They must . . . They must know. . . . Judy! No wonder he didn't follow me. They'll be at the hotel. They'll . . .

In a moment he was out in the street again, surprised to see two workmen on the opposite side of the road lighting cigarettes. He began to run. The damp paper packet of food thumped against his ribs.

—Hurry, he thought. Hurry, hurry, in time with the slapping of his feet. His lungs were like sheet rubber stretched across his chest.

Yet nobody turned to stare at him as he passed. Not the old people in black nor the strong young men with cropped hair, nor the girls with short skirts lounging against their mopeds.

Arriving at the street where the hotel was, he stopped and heard the echo of his flight.

—Hurry. Hurry.

A cat sloped from the hotel steps and moved away from him, its tail erect. Otherwise there was no one. He walked to the hotel.

Inside the lobby there was coolness, a smell of damp plaster, the glint of metal key rings on a board behind the desk. He climbed the stairs. At the door of the room he stopped and listened. There might be men in a semicircle waiting with guns. There might be a freshly made bed, a polished floor, clean towels by the basin.

Entering and seeing Judy lying on the bed, he felt an emptiness in himself.

—You scared me. I didn't hear you come in. Where've you been all this time?

—Here.

Graham handed her the brown paper packet. She did not take it and it fell on the bedspread beside her.

—Where on earth have you been? I thought you'd got lost or something.

Graham went to the basin and drank from the cold tap. The water tasted bitter. It fell out of his mouth and across his chin. The sweat was drying inside his shirt.

—Well, tell me. What's happened? Obviously something happened.

—Nobody's been here? asked Graham.

He looked out of the window. The street at midday was like a skeleton.

—Of course not.

—That's all right then, he said. Aren't you hungry anymore?

He pointed to the parcel.

—Go on. Open it.

Judy held the parcel up and tipped its contents onto the bed. She said:

—That looks good.

Then she said:

—Tell me.

Graham sat beside her. He slit open the packet of salami with his thumbnail. He thought:

—If I tell her she'll be frightened.

He also thought:

—If I tell her she'll laugh at me.

He said:

—There was a slight problem with the police.

—What? What sort . . . ?

—Nothing much, he said. It's all right now.

—What happened?

—I was being followed. Look, do you want to eat or not?

She took three slices of the sausage and folded them. She ate them, pulling the skin away from the meat with her teeth.

—I noticed . . . , said Graham. I just noticed, in the supermarket, that I was being watched. That's all. I knew he was a policeman and then, when he followed me out, I was certain.

—But . . . ?

—Well, I couldn't come straight back here, now could I? So I . . . I led him another way. Walking. Quite naturally. And I managed to lose him, in the back streets. Then I waited to make sure and then I came back to you. They don't know where you are. It's quite all right.

—But . . . ?

—Come on.

He took the Camembert from its box and broke it in two. The white center dribbled over the lip of the cheese.

—Quickly. Before it runs everywhere.

The girl ate, not wanting to eat. She said:

100

—How did they . . . ? I mean, they're not after *you.* I don't understand.

—Look, I don't know any more than you do, said Graham. But obviously . . . For heaven's sake, we've been seen together. We left Benmel in the car together. Of course they know.

—What do we do?

—Nothing. We'll stick to our original plan.

The girl said:

—I'm going to hand myself in.

—You're not, said Graham and immediately wished that he had not answered so quickly. It almost sounded as though he had anticipated her remark, had conjured it up himself.

—I am, Graham. It's the only thing to do.

—You mustn't. You can't. Not now.

—Please! I can't . . . and besides, this way you needn't be involved.

—You don't think I've gone this far just to . . . ?

—Please.

—No, he said. No.

—If you do what I ask you we'll be all right. Just trust me, Judy, will you? The important thing is to get you out of France and as soon as we can. Tomorrow you'll be safe. Tomorrow everything'll be all right.

—In a few hours.

—In a few hours it'll all be over, said Graham.

—Then up come the lights and we can all go home, said Judy.

101

12

There was still the question of the passport.

The photograph in Judy's passport was not stamped and in Avignon Graham had promised that he would do something about this, although now he was not quite so certain that it was necessary, was not quite so certain that he knew how he should do it.

The stamp, as Graham could see from his own, was not a simple one, being made up of the words "Foreign and Commonwealth Office" surrounding the royal coat of arms. Neither was it reproduced in ink but impressed into the paper so that the lettering stood out in bas-relief.

—How are you going to copy that? Judy asked.

It was two o'clock. Through the half-closed shutters the hotel bedroom was the color of cream.

—It shouldn't be too hard, said Graham.

He turned on the hot tap and held the page for a moment under it.

—What are you doing? Won't the photograph come un-stuck?

—Not if I'm careful, said Graham, pressing down the curling corner of the photograph.

—Now . . .

He searched around for something. A pin perhaps. Too sharp. Might tear the paper.

—A paintbrush, he said. In the box in my suitcase. The smallest one you can find. And a rag.

He placed a clean corner of the rag on top of the photo-graph and, turning the page, began to draw, mirror-fash-ion, on the back of the damp paper with the handle of his brush.

It was not easy. The paper dried quickly in the heat so that he had several times to remoisten it but he was work-ing, enjoying the feel of varnished wood between his fingers, the concentration of the hunched back. The girl stood close to him and in his mind she smelled of pine resin and the sea.

When he had finished he laid the passport on the win-dowsill.

—It's hardly perfect, he said, but it'll do. They won't look that closely. It's not as though they're English.

—I think it's fantastic, said Judy.

—It'll do.

Now he felt tired. The day had become muggy and there was thunder behind the heat. He took a cigarette and lit it.

—Can I have one? said the girl.

—What? he said.

—Could I have a smoke?

He said:

—You don't smoke.

—Sometimes. Not often.

—Of course.

Why had he thought that she did not smoke? He remembered now the way that she held cigarettes with her lips and drew the smoke deep into her lungs, like a . . .

—You shouldn't smoke, you know, he said.

—You can't talk.

—No . . .

He had not meant that.

He gave her a cigarette and turned from her. He sat on the bed. He lay on the bed and saw the bodies of flies caught in a web around the ceiling rose.

The ship for Oran did not leave until half-past nine. Six and a half more hours. There should have been an earlier ship but what could he do?

—We'll go as soon as it starts to get dark, he said.

—What do we do till then?

He did not know. He had not thought about this.

—Cards? she said.

—I haven't got any.

—But . . . ?

—Those? They belonged to the children.

The children.

Judy said:

—I expect they'll be back at school by now. Jean-Marc must be quite a hero.

—I expect so.

He was remembering the way they used to cling to his

neck at night when he went to tuck them up, the way they had smelled—of sand and cotton and toffee, the roughness of their arms, how they had said:

—Don't leave us. Stay with us.

And how, returning hours later on the way to bed himself, he would find them lying on their backs with clenched fists raised to their faces, asleep, not needing anybody.

—I expect he'll forget all about it, he said. Once the plasters have come off and the bone's mended. Children don't think back. Or forward, I suppose. Even the present seems a bit unreal with them, doesn't it? As if they're seeing it through some kind of distorted mirror made of their dreams and their games. They're very . . . subjective.

—Selfish, said the girl. I've always thought kids were very selfish.

—Oh, no. Well . . . in a way but . . . it's not *wrong*, for them. Is it?

—I don't know. I suppose they just don't know any better.

—Well, who's to say what's *better*? I don't think we're really in a position to judge.

Graham found that he was angry although the argument was not important.

—We're seeing it from our standpoint, aren't we? Assuming that things automatically get better as they get older, that people do. I mean, it might not be like that at all. Every day we might be moving further and further away from the truth.

—What truth?

—I don't know, but . . . Oh, it doesn't matter.

105

The girl said:

—You like children, don't you?

—Yes, he said. No, I think I admire them.

—Admire them?

—Well . . .

The ball of dead flies suspended from the ceiling rose turned. A breeze must have blown up. He said:

—I'm not sure if I understand them, really.

—Have you never had any? said the girl.

—Never.

The way he said it the word sounded final.

Of course it had been impossible with Miranda. They had not been married and, as he had pointed out, whatever liberal ideas she might have on the subject of illegitimacy, it would hardly have been fair on the child. Then she had said:

—Well, why don't we get married then? I mean, we're as good as, aren't we?

But he had been frightened that she would feel trapped if they did. Instead he had suggested that she get a coil fitted.

One day she had it removed but still nothing happened. After that the subject was not mentioned by them.

And now . . .

He had never felt the need to reproduce himself. He told people, he told himself, that his paintings were his legacy to another generation, his work justified his existence. That the decision might now, however, have been taken out of his hands irritated him. He said:

—Look, let's take a nap, hey? A siesta.

—I'm not tired. In any case, I don't think I could sleep this afternoon.

—No.

She said:

—I'm sorry. I mean, if I was getting too personal.

—Oh! No, of course you weren't, he said.

He looked at his watch. The hands stood at ten past three. Six hours and twenty minutes to go.

Graham thought:

—These are the dangerous hours: the hours that lie between the doing of things.

—I know what we'll do, he said. We'll play picture consequences, like you used to do with them. You'll see I'm not much good at it. And if we get bored with that we'll play . . . battleships. Anything, anything.

—O.K., said Judy.

In the sagging hotel room with its dead flies and its striped half-light through the shutters, they played games and kept their thoughts to themselves until it was dark.

—I think we can go now, said Graham.

The night had come without warning and now he was not sure that it had not come too soon. Somehow he had not had time to prepare himself for the important thing that was about to happen: the climax to his adventure.

He took Judy's passport from the windowsill and gave it to her. There were people in the street. None of them was watching the hotel.

He put the cellophane wrappers with their remains of cold meat and cheese into the wastepaper basket under the basin. Also the empty wine bottle.

—You'd better wear a coat, he said to the girl.

—I haven't got one.

He took a sweater from his suitcase.

—Take this, he said.

—It's all right.

—Go on. It'll be cold tonight.

She put the sweater on under her suit jacket. It engulfed her and she looked small. Graham remembered that when he was eighteen he had been to a dance and in the garden, behind the tennis court, a girl had worn his dinner jacket.

He said:

—That's it then. All right?

—Fine.

—We haven't left anything?

He checked just to make sure. He liked to leave places as he had found them. He folded the towels and hung them on the bar beside the basin.

—Come on then.

It was eight o'clock. In a room off the lobby people were eating. They heard their voices as they passed and the clatter of their knives.

Outside they got into the car and drove through cobbled side streets, through palm-treed squares, to the docks. There they parked.

—Right, said Graham. Now, there are one or two things . . .

He took a folded wad of notes from his pocket and gave

it to the girl. He knew how much was in it. There was as much as he could afford to give her without depriving himself.

—Oh, no, she said. I can't take all . . .

—Come on. I owe it to you in any case.

—Not all this.

—Besides, you'll need it. Until you can find yourself some kind of job. Though that shouldn't be hard when . . . when you . . . I mean, there you'll be able to . . .

There was something he meant to say to her.

He looked at her, sitting beside him upright in the car. Her fists were cupped one inside the other on her lap. Her face was immobile, expressionless, as it had been once before when he had tried to draw it. Her eyebrows were thick and her nose was too large but her lips were soft and full and her eyes, her hair, the short hairs that crested her cheekbones, were white-gold in the lights of the harbor. Seeing her like this it was hard to remember what he had meant to say.

Half-knowing, however, he forced himself to look at her legs. They were clothed in stockings now and shadowed in the dark beneath the dashboard. Only the knees shone like naked ivory, tight under the stretch of nylon, angular like the knees of a schoolboy.

—When you get there, he said, you'll be able to . . .

He looked ahead of him through the windscreen. On the quay lorries turned and irregular tides of people moved. Behind them towered the massive gray breasts of the boats.

—One of those is yours, he said. I suppose we'd better go and find it.

He gave her her ticket.

—You'll need this too, he said.

He took the key from the ignition. He took her case from the back seat. When she had left the car he locked her door, got out and joined her.

The heat of the day had dispersed, giving way to an evening that was neither hot nor cold, and as they walked the air that surrounded them was an unsettling mixture of stillness, of wordless voices, of the smells of frying and of the invisible sea. They walked, both of them, with their shoulders hunched.

The customs shed was a large, hollow building with the desolate feel of all places where people come only in order to go somewhere else. Yet it had a life, a kind of excitable, false energy engendered by those it contained: the Arabs with their gray jibbas and their tired gray faces, the clusters of students, the middle-aged couples fussing over their luggage, the businessmen, the traders, all of them charged with that special quality which is the traveler's alone.

Those who had come merely to see friends off recognized this and stood aside, embarrassed, in a position resembling that of worship, their heads bowed, their hands clasped before their lower stomach.

A port official exchanged Judy's ticket for an embarkation card. Graham bought a boarding pass.

As they left the shed he noticed that the girl was trembling and then her fear transmitted itself to him, like an emotion disjointed through water, so that he found that he too was shaking—not with fear but with excitement. The end of his adventure was in sight and he was enjoying the sweet tension of the protracted climax.

110

In silence they walked along the water's edge to where the ship pulled, her gangplank already thick with passengers. Those who had boarded her leaned against the deck railings and stared down at the quay, their minds, like their bodies, already in a no man's land between this place with its name and another called something else.

At the top of the gangplank Graham could see two customs officers collecting cards, checking passports, asking routine questions. He noted that they showed a perfunctory interest in their job, the greater part of their concentration being taken up with a private joke of some length and involvement.

—This shouldn't be too bad, he thought.

He stood aside to let the girl go before him. She hesitated. She said:

—Well . . . good-bye.

—I'm coming up with you. I've got to make sure you get on safely.

—Don't, she said. I'll be O.K.

—Nonsense.

They were standing on the bottom step. The people behind them were impatient to be getting on. So they began to climb, the girl first, then Graham.

And as they climbed, as the queue before them shortened and the crowd behind them thickened, as step by step they moved, were moved, toward the two men in uniform, Graham at last began to feel frightened. Not the heart-pounding, breath-catching frightened of a game but real fear, fear that numbed his mouth and darkened his eyesight, fear that thickened his hearing so that all he knew was a voice inside his head saying, softly at first:

—It's you, Graham. It's you they're after. When they see that stamp you forged it won't just be Judy they'll want. It'll be you. You've committed a crime. You're an accessory after the fact. You're helping a murderer. And, Graham, there's no way down.

Then, louder:

—They'll get you, Graham. They'll get you. You, Graham. You, you, you.

He stopped.

He turned.

The rope handrail became taut beneath his weight.

People were watching him. Down the gangplank a column of tilted faces watched him. On the quay a hundred pairs of eyes were trained on him.

—Don't panic, he said. He might have said it out loud.

—Don't panic!

Once more he scanned the faces below him. They passed across his vision like a vortex of fairground lights, making him feel dizzy.

Yet when he saw the small, fat man with the large forehead he did not fall.

13

He stood some way off, beyond the crowd that thronged the harbor's edge, beyond the customs shed, leaning against a crisscross wire fence, his head illuminated from above by a single lamp. He wore the same blue suit that he had worn in the supermarket. It was as though it was the only one he possessed, a part of him, his distinguishing feature.

Graham saw him and knew that he had never really expected to see him again, not in the street outside the hotel, not here either. For a moment he could not believe it. Then the man moved a few steps so that his shadow swung out large around him, and he said something to a sailor standing nearby. Then Graham had to believe.

In that moment he put his hand to the mirror and found that it was not made of glass. What he had done was not a game. And this realization, this one fact, was the trigger that ignited the explosive inside him. Through the storm in his head one light said:

—You must get away.

There were prisons and trials and newspaper headlines. There was degradation and a life thrown away. But if he ran. If he ran fast . . .

Not alone though. He would not run alone. The girl must come with him. He saw in that moment of terror what he had not seen before and what he would immediately forget: that the girl was fulfilling a purpose and that that purpose was not yet over. Through her his adventure had come into existence and with her it must end. He could not let her escape to an unknown conclusion.

There is a shape to art and the creator cannot stop his work until an answer has been achieved, for he can be certain that the creation will not allow itself to peter out into a row of dots but will find its own resolution.

Having understood this, Graham turned it into words and said:

—I can't just run out on her. I've got to stand by her to the end.

He turned. She was a few steps above him now. He saw that she had reached the top of the gangplank, that she was talking to the customs officers. They had her passport. They were turning the pages.

—Judy!

The two men in uniform looked at him. He was stumbling toward them.

The girl looked at him.

—It's all right, she said, from a long way above.

114

—No, it's not. He's there. He's down there.

—Who?

Run. They had to run. Why couldn't she see that they had to run?

—*Qu'est-ce qu'il y a?* asked one of the officers.

—No, said Judy. It's quite all right.

—Judy, they know. Let me have that passport, please.

—*Pourquoi?* What is the matter?

—*Donnez-le-moi.* Judy, get down.

—Graham, it's all O.K. They haven't . . .

—They know, I tell you. Come down.

—Graham!

She did not move so he took her arm and pulled her toward him. She fell and, half carrying her, he pushed his way past the other passengers, who screamed and shouted, falling back against the unsteady ropes.

The officers called:

—Stop! *Arrêtez-vous!* But did not follow them.

They reached the ground and he began to run, across the tarmac, through the customs shed, toward the car.

But the car was separated from them by a small expanse of wasteland and in the middle of this area, walking as though concerned in quite another matter, was the man from the supermarket.

—Hell!

Graham dropped the girl's suitcase. He looked around. To his right were the bustle and lights of the Gare Maritime, ahead and to his left, warehouses.

—This way, he said. Quick. Quickly.

115

They ran again. Behind him Graham could hear the beating of the girl's shoes, the rasping of her breath.

In a minute they had left the open space and were moving along dark passages on either side of which rose the high walls of the warehouses, heavy with the damp smells of spices and meat. Down one of these lanes Graham stopped. They had come to a flight of wooden steps leading from the ground to a door halfway up the building face. The door was ajar and no light came from it.

—Up here, he said.

There was great excitement aboard the ship *Kailiman*.

Those passengers who had witnessed the incredible scene of a man dragging a young girl from the very top of the gangplank found themselves the center of attention as those less fortunate than they gathered round to hear each event told, retold, exaggerated, in a babel of languages.

—It was the police, of course. She's the leader of a famous drug ring. They say . . .

—Her husband. Trying to stop her running off with a sheik.

—Her lover.

—Her father.

—Kidnappers. With guns.

Only the customs officers remained impervious to the commotion. They shrugged their shoulders and shouted at the passengers from time to time, without anger.

When the last of these had been bustled aboard, the last

116

rope untied, the last whistle blown and the rusty hulk of the *Kailiman* began once more to sail out of the harbor forty-three minutes late, they made their way to their supervisor's office and told him what had happened.

—You've still got the passport? he said.

—But yes, sir. They ran off, like that, without it.

—Then give it to me, you idiots.

—Yes, sir. The whole thing was very strange, sir.

—No doubt. You didn't think to stop them?

—Well, no. There were people and . . .

—Quite.

It did not take the supervisor long to discover the forgery. Having done so he at once reported the matter to the chief of the harbor police.

—It seems that she was trying to use someone else's passport, said this latter, after some time.

—So it would appear. But why?

—Maybe they'll have the answer at the gendarmerie.

—Do we need to bother them?

—Of course. It might be important. You never know. Leave it with me.

Commissaire Tourot was tired. His office, which in winter could never be induced to reach a temperature of more than fifteen degrees centigrade, in summer clung stubbornly to the heat of the day so that even at this late hour his shirt stuck to his back and the smoke from a hundred untipped Gitanes lay low in the air, drying his throat, irritating his eyes. He had been at work since after lunch.

He greeted the chief of the harbor police with some impatience.

—Well, Masse, what's the problem now?

—I'm not sure that it is a problem. But perhaps you'll just look at this, will you?

He put Judy Keeble's passport down on the commissaire's desk and told him the story behind it. The commissaire listened. When it was finished he tilted back in his chair and said:

—So.

Seeing that he was not disinterested, the chief of the harbor police said:

—This Judy Keeble. She means something to you?

—No, said the commissaire.

He ran his hand round the inside of his collar.

—No.

He said:

—There was a man with her, this girl? You said something about a man.

—Yes. It was a man who dragged her away. English also.

—Young?

—No, not young. I told you. A middle-aged man.

The chief of the harbor police would have liked a seat but none was offered him. He looked at the notices on the wall behind the commissaire's desk and wondered whether he should leave or stay, make a suggestion or keep quiet. It was hard to tell with the commissaire. Years of interviewing prisoners had left Tourot with few social niceties. He

118

treated conversation as a poker game. When he did speak he said:

—Well, thank you.

—Is that all?

—I think you can leave this to us.

—Yes. Well . . . I thought it was more your problem than ours.

The chief of the harbor police replaced his cap and went toward the door.

—One moment! said the commissaire.

—Yes?

—I suppose nobody tried to stop them?

—Stop them? Well, no. They hadn't done anything wrong.

—Forging a passport?

—That . . . You understand I wasn't present when this all took place . . . but I believe that the—er—stamp was not noticed until later.

—Not by the customs officials?

—No. . . .

—It's a forgery of quiet alarming amateurism. Wouldn't you say?

—Yes. Quite. Quite. I shall see that the men concerned . . .

· —And yet if it hadn't been noticed I wonder why they . . . ?

The commissaire leaned forward across the desk, his large, calloused hands splayed palms downward before him. At last he said:

—That'll be all, Masse. You may go.

When the chief of the harbor police had left, Commissaire Tourot lifted the receiver of his desk telephone and called for a sergeant to come to him.

—Yes, sir?

—We received a communication the other day, said the commissaire, from Interpol, you remember? About an Englishman wanted in London for murdering his wife. They had reason to think he might be in this country.

—Yes, sir. I remember. Robin Howard.

—Robin Howard. And the wife. The murdered wife. What was she called?

—I can't . . .

—Might it have been Judy Keeble?

—Yes. Yes, sir, I think that was it.

Commissaire Tourot pushed the passport with its photograph across the top of his desk.

—Is this Judy Keeble or Robin Howard? he asked.

They got the Interpol communication on Robin Howard from its file. They compared photographs. Within minutes all relevant information and pictures had been circulated to mobile police forces in the city and around.

A description of the wanted man's companion, however, was not so easy to come by.

—He was English.

Everyone who had seen him was certain of that. But . . .

—What age was he?

—Middle-aged. Thirty-five, forty-five, fifty-five.

—Height?

—Medium.

—Coloring?

—Well . . . fair. Darkish fair.

—His face? Any peculiarities?

—None. Quite good looking. Quite ordinary looking. Quite English.

As to whether the couple had left by car or on foot, nobody could be found who knew for certain. Someone said that he had seen them running toward the warehouses. Another had seen them drive off in a red sports car.

The commissaire informed London of what had happened.

Then he lit a cigarette, poured himself a glass of three-star cognac from the bottle in his bottom drawer and walked over to the window of his office. He pressed down a slat of the yellowed Venetian blind. Across the road a clock said twenty-five past eleven.

—Well, they're out there somewhere, he thought. And we'll get them. Murderers—those kind—they're nearly always amateurs. People who couldn't get away with shoplifting, jumping traffic lights. Wouldn't dream of it, probably.

He sipped his brandy. The hot liquid circled his mouth and slid like flames to his stomach. He had done all he could for the moment but there were still one or two questions that bothered him.

This older man, for instance, who was he? How far was he involved? Did he and the boy have some kind of homosexual relationship? They were, after all, English.

And then, less important, more puzzling, why had they panicked like that at the last minute? What unguessable stupidity had made them run when in a few minutes they would have been safe, on their way to countries where criminals can be lost forever in a desert of unexplained faces, of questionable pasts?

—That's what we'll never know, thought Commissaire Tourot. That's what nobody'll think to ask.

He allowed the Venetian blind to snap back into place. A cloud of dust unsettled itself.

—Ah, well. It's not important. The man committed a murder and we'll arrest him. Tomorrow. Next year. Those are the facts. Murder, rape, theft, traffic jams. Getting up in the morning and going to work and eating and drinking and fucking. Those are the facts.

He tilted his glass so that the last drops of gold washed up the concave sides and trickled over his tongue.

—No, he thought. I'd as soon leave it to the psychiatrists and the social workers to fathom what goes on in the minds of their fellow-men, if they can. If they think it's worthwhile. Imagination's a harmless enough thing after all. In an empty room it's impotent. And most people, thank God, contrive to live their lives in empty rooms. Or, in any case, nurseries full of harmless toys. It's only when the mind that's got greed or anger or despair in it finds itself attached to a hand with a gun in it that I have to worry.

He took his jacket from the back of his chair. It was time for him to go home.

—That's the trouble, he said. That's the trouble. When fact and fantasy somehow get joined together.

He left the office.

—Any news yet, sergeant?

122

—Not yet, sir. But we'll get them.

—Good night then.

—Good night, sir.

Commissaire Tourot got into his car.

—Fact and fantasy, he said. Like dry grass and a match. Separate—nothing. Together, a mountain on fire.

14

The darkness was complete.

Not at the corners did it fray into grayness, nor indeed *were* there any corners, merely black without end until the outstretched hand touched flaking plaster and withdrew. Above, below and around them the silence was a wadding that stifled both breath and heartbeat. In their throats crept the sickness of dead flesh from the floor below. A tanners' warehouse, where the skins of animals toughened to leather and the meat rotted.

For a quarter of an hour after entering this place they had stood in silence, protected only by the treacherous darkness, waiting for the opening of a door, for the flash of a torch that would discover them like clowns in a circus ring with no trousers on.

During this time they had not moved.

Graham had felt no need to move. His body had been nerveless as though, having run so fast and well at his mind's behest, it was now incapable of any other action.

When no footsteps passed the warehouse, however, or followed theirs up the wooden steps against the wall, when he had become accustomed to the totality of the silence, he said:

—We've done it.

—What?

The word followed his own so rapidly that the statement and question were as one.

—We've . . .

Graham could not see the girl nor calculate from her voice where she was.

—Where are you? he said.

She did not answer.

He opened his eyes wide as though by staring harder he could make the black less black.

—Judy? he said.

Still she did not answer.

For a moment he thought:

—Perhaps she's gone, and could not explain the relief he felt.

—Judy?

—Oh, stop it.

—What?

—Do you have to go on calling me that?

He said:

—Are you all right?

—Of course I'm not all right.

He heard her moving now and saw the darkness move, showing him where she was.

—I didn't hurt you, did I? he said.

—Hurt me?

125

—I might've been a bit rough . . .

He was turning on the spot, led by the circle of her footfall.

She said:

—Why the hell did you do it, Graham? I just don't know what you're playing at. I was there. I was so bloody nearly there . . .

She stopped because she was crying.

—Judy . . .

He felt for her in the dark.

—Don't touch me. And don't call me that.

—I'm sorry, said Graham.

He withdrew his hand.

—I'm sorry.

He did not know why he was apologizing. The words were no more than the incantation of a childhood religion, the mea culpa that his lips knew better than his heart.

—Mummy, Mummy, look what I've done. I'm so awfully sorry.

—That's all right, darling. As long as you know you've been naughty.

Words formed in his mouth and his body moved. His mind, for the moment, stood still.

From nearer to him now and not crying, the girl said:

—Why did you do it?

—I don't . . .

He could not understand her question. He knew that they were safe, that they had run and were safe.

—We're safe, he said.

—You're safe, maybe.

Again her voice answered his before he knew that he had spoken.

—And I *was* all right. They were just going to let me on the ship. It would've been all over. For you it would. I thought that was what you wanted.

—Wanted?

He wanted her to touch him, to tell him with her hands that they were all right. Not this.

—Didn't you? she said. Didn't you want to get it over with?

Graham could see her now—her shadow in the shadow.

—That's what I thought, she said.

—I don't know. . . .

—Then why did you muck it up like that? What happened?

Graham remembered that there had been a man with a blue suit.

—The police . . . , he said.

—What do you mean?

—The man . . .

He reached behind him for a wall to lean against and found nothing. He said:

—The man who followed me the other day. This morning, I mean. . . .

—You saw him?

—Yes.

—At the port?

—Yes.

That he knew.

—Yes. He was on the quay. The same man. Watching me.

—And?

—Don't you see? They must have known about you.

—You can't be sure of that.

—We had to run away.

—But we didn't, we didn't. It was the one thing we had not to do. That's the whole point. We were taking a risk but we knew that, didn't we? And now we're bound to be caught. We haven't a chance. Oh, Graham, why? When I trusted you.

She cried again, with drawn-out, vocalized sobs that defiled the sanctity of the darkness.

—Shhh, said Graham. Be quiet. Someone'll hear you.

—*I don't care.*

The echo of her cry died slowly in the black sickness that surrounded them.

Graham put his head between his hands. He, too, was near to tears. He thought:

—It's not fair. It's not fair. I didn't want this.

He thought:

—If only I could sleep.

The girl kept moving. He wanted to forget her but she dislocated the darkness with her movement. Her feet were heavy on the floorboards. He wanted to say:

—Stay still!

He wanted to say:

—Shut up! Please shut up!

Her presence was like a sore festering inside his brain. He would have scratched it out with his nails. It was as though she had become a part of him: a horrible, tumor-ridden limb that must be amputated before it killed him.

128

And he realized, with the certainty with which one realizes something that one has always known, that he no longer wanted the girl to exist.

It was as simple as that.

Were she part of a painting he would have eradicated her.

This thought, this feeling rather, was so enormous that at first Graham could not accept it. He tried instead to think of other things. He said:

—We're going to have to . . .

His voice was empty. He said:

—We're going to have to make some new plans now, aren't we?

—I suppose so, said the girl, behind him.

—I . . . I think the best thing to do is . . .

—What? she said. Go on, what do you suggest? We won't even be able to leave the town now. They've got my passport, remember. They know just what they're looking for.

—Oh, I shouldn't think . . .

—Don't be stupid. It's for real now, Graham.

—Hasn't it always been? he said.

—Has it?

She was near him now. He could smell her breath, taste her spittle on his lips, see the half-halo of her hair.

—Of course it has, he said. Now, listen . . .

—No.

—What?

—I'm not going to listen. I think I've done quite enough of that, don't you? I think it's time that I had some say in my life. You just don't . . .You've got no idea what it's been

like. Oh, I . . . Graham, listen. *You* listen. I've killed somebody. There. I can't quite believe it myself. I mean, I say
it, I tell you about it, I put it into words but I don't believe
it. And you! It really has all been a game to you.

—That's not true.

—But it is! Oh, hell! I don't even know why you wanted
to help me in the first place. I thought . . . I don't know what
I thought. I mean, when I met you I really was resigned to
being caught. I never thought I could get away with what
I'd done. And then . . . Oh, well, you were older than me
and you seemed so competent and I suppose I just clutched
at this stupid hope. I was mad, of course. I should have
guessed it would end like this.

—You can't just give up.

—I'm a murderer. Why in God's name won't you listen
to me? It's not like in a whodunit, you know. You don't just
do something like that and then cold-bloodedly plan how
you're going to get away with it. You don't want to get away
with it. That's the horrible truth.

—That's stupid.

—No, it's not. It's not. It's just the way people are. You
haven't got the slightest idea.

—I'm a person too, for heaven's sake.

Graham was finding it difficult to breathe. The stench of
decaying meat lay thick on his throat and in the pit of his
stomach. The girl's words, so unexpected, somehow so
familiar, beat at him like a flail. He felt powerless. He
fought the sensation but did not mind that he was losing
the fight, knowing, perhaps, that in the end he could not
lose, being on the frontier of an old truth about creating
and destroying.

The girl continued:

—I don't blame you or anything. I don't suppose it's your fault. You can't help being the way you are. It's just that it was so important and now, somehow, it's turned into a pathetic game of hide and seek.

—What would you have done without me?

He spoke the words not waiting for an answer. Not waiting for an answer to that question.

—I don't know but . . . at least it would have been over sooner. I didn't ask you to help me.

—What else could I have done?

—Anything. Reported me to the police. Ignored me.

—I couldn't.

—Of course you could.

—No, said Graham.

This was important. He said:

—I did the only thing I could do. I did the best I could. If it hasn't worked, I'm sorry.

—Don't be sorry.

She had moved away from him. He could no longer see her at all, not even a disturbance in the blackness. He could only hear her voice, muffled, as though her back were to him. She said:

—In any case it doesn't matter. It's all over now.

—Almost, almost, thought Graham.

In a minute it would be over. All he had to do was find the key to the door he had locked. It was there. It was there somewhere, entangled in the mesh of words that stretched between them in the darkness.

He said:

—We've still got a chance. We can still do it, Judy.

131

And the door flew open.

She might have seen it too for she waited a long time before saying:

—My name's Robin. Robin Howard. Judy Keeble's dead.

15

—You'd better go, said the boy. By yourself you'll probably stand a chance. Go on. It'll be safer for me as well. They're looking for two of us, remember.

It was four o'clock.

They had slept a bit and had woken to find the morning graying through a dusty skylight. They had not realized that in their hiding place were empty sacks piled loosely against a wall and crates with wire fastenings.

—Yes. You're right, said Graham. We'd better separate.

He did not look at the boy.

He went to the door and opened it. The air from the open corridor below was sharp and bit at his breath. There were no sounds. From the west, from the port, came the dull orange glow of artificial light suspended from the night. In the east the day was uncertain and raw.

—Where will you go? he said.

—I don't know, said the boy. Somewhere. I . . .

—You've got the money.

—Yes. Would you . . .

—No, said Graham.

—O.K., said the boy.

Graham closed the door, although there was nothing left to do now but to leave. The triangle of his neck and chest burned from the cold outside. Within the warehouse it was warm and the stink from the dead flesh below was like a comfortable remembering.

He pushed his hands into his jeans pockets, where fluff and tobacco strands caught beneath his nails. Still he did not look at the boy. He said:

—Which one of us'll go first?

—It doesn't matter.

—Well, let's go down together in any case. Then we can split up after that.

He listened for the footfall behind him. He reopened the door.

Against the side of the building the wooden steps glistened with dew frost and when he trod on them they were slippery to his feet. He descended slowly, touching the brickwork with the flat of his left hand. At the bottom he stopped and said:

—Well, then . . .

But one end of the passage was blocked off by a blank wall so they walked together toward the other opening. Then Graham stopped again. Before them and around them loomed the dark, dank sides of the warehouses. Beyond them, in front of them, was the sea. Graham heard water slurping. Close at hand a ship's siren groaned and for a while the sound hung there, doubly lonely in the enclosing stillness. Then a church clock tolled the half-hour and was echoed by others further and further away. Neither the town nor the sea was asleep. Merely waiting.

Graham thought:

—This is it, then. We have reached an end. Now at last we shall be by ourselves again.

He narrowed his eyes and peered into the gloom, looking for nothing. He said:

—Well, then, old boy. Which way?

—I don't mind.

—Well, no. Nor do I. Um . . .

—Just go.

—O.K.

It was so easy and yet he could not bring himself to leave, not without turning and saying something, some sort of unnecessary good-bye. Nor could he bring himself to turn.

—What's keeping you? said the boy.

—Nothing. Nothing.

—Then for God's sake hurry.

—I will. I shall.

They heard the footsteps in the same moment. Or rather, Graham felt the boy stiffen and then he heard them: even, unhurried, a man's footsteps somewhere very close to them, either to the right or to the left.

—God! said Graham.

—Run! said the boy.

—Let's go back.

—Not now.

135

The boy pushed past Graham and ran down one of the passages.

—*Qui va?* called a voice.

The footsteps to which the voice belonged lengthened and began to run too. The noise of them reverberated from high wall to high wall until it sounded as though they were everywhere, as though there were not a black corner nor obscure alleyway that could escape their heavy beat.

—Judy! called Graham.

The footsteps answered:

—*Arrêtez-vous! C'est la police!*

A whistle blew and Graham found that he was moving also, although he could not feel his legs and his eyes were blurred. The road was tilting. The road disappeared. His heart in his head was saying:

—Not me. Not me. Not me.

When he saw the police car draw up he sank to his knees and joined his hands together behind his neck.

In separate cars they drove them to the gendarmerie and there shut them in separate cells.

—We'll leave that little lot for the commissaire to deal with, the sergeant on night duty said in French.

—Shouldn't we ring him?

—It'll keep till morning. They won't get away now.

It had never occurred to Graham that a real prison would have bars. He had imagined them to be a cinematic convention, like crooks with pencil mustaches or homicidal butlers. Now their presence comforted him. Their absurd association with files smuggled in in sponge cakes reassured him.

He was glad of the policeman watching him from the desk at the end of the row so that he dared not touch them and discover their reality.

In the next cell the boy slept, or pretended to sleep, lying on his stomach, his face turned to the whitewashed bricks.

Graham was glad of this also. He needed an aloneness in which not to think, a vacuum to suffocate conjecture. There was a luxury in unquestioned hopelessness at last.

Throughout the long dawn he sat upright, silent on his uncomfortable mattress. He held his knees to his chest and his interlaced fingers did not move. He stared without blinking past the tiled passageway, past the rounded arch and the sepia-faced, Roman-numbered clock, past the sergeant's desk where men came to throw down their kepis and scratch their hair and smoke their loosely packed cheroots.

He did not see the night sergeant leave. He did not hear when the replacement called Commissaire Tourot on the telephone and informed him of the capture. He did not notice, fifteen minutes later, the commissaire's hurried arrival.

Waiting outside his headmaster's study once, for a beating he had not deserved, he had thrown back his head like this and stared through a mullioned window, while outside boys played cricket or walked arm-over-shoulder to tea knowing nothing of his solitary courage.

137

—*Alors*, said the young gendarme. *Dépêchez-vous.* Quickly, please.

He had unlocked both cell doors and now stood back against the wall clinking his keys. He was not sure if the foreigners had understood him.

—Quickly, please, he repeated. *Monsieur le Commissaire veut vous voir.* The commissaire shall see you.

He was twenty. His wide, flat face was flushed with freckles and he shifted like a crab from one boot to the other.

—Come now, he said.

—Both of us? said Graham in French.

He had not anticipated this, that they should both go in together.

—But yes, said the young man in uniform. Hurry up, please.

—Of course, said Graham.

When he stood up his head hummed.

He had not anticipated this. He had been certain that they would be questioned separately, that he would be able to stand alone before the policeman and say:

—I accept whatever punishment you give me.

He had *known* it would be like that.

Yet a few feet away from him, as seen in an unexpected mirror, someone else was getting up from a mattress in a prison cell. A ridiculous figure. A boy in a woman's suit. A boy whose stockinged legs wrinkled, whose face—perched

138

between two sexes—achieved neither, whose eyes were dirty with makeup, whose chin was untidy with beard.

—Who is he? thought Graham.

He knew.

—Then what does he want with me? He's nothing to do with me. I knew someone else. This person is pathetic.

Again he said to the young gendarme:

—Both of us?

—I said yes. Now come.

He pulled Graham by the sleeve.

—Leave me, said Graham.

He wished to walk with dignity.

At the door to the commissaire's office the young gendarme stopped and knocked.

—*Entrez,* said a voice.

—Graham, the boy behind him said.

—What?

He did not turn.

—Graham, there's no need for you to . . . Will you leave it to me?

—No, said Graham.

They went into the office.

—Thank you, officer, said Commissaire Tourot to the young gendarme.

And in English:

—Good morning, gentlemen.

—Good morning, said Graham in French.

—Will you sit? said the commissaire, in English.

He indicated two wooden chairs.

139

To the boy he said:

—Robin Howard?

—Yes, said the boy.

—Quite so, said the commissaire.

He stood up and took something from the top drawer of his desk.

—I believe this is your passport, he said.

—It's my wife's, said the boy.

—Your late wife's. You did know that your wife had been murdered, Mr. Howard?

—You know I do.

—Do I?

—Oh, look. I'm not trying to deny it. I did it. I killed her. Only, please . . .

He looked at Graham.

—Yes? said the commissaire.

He moved back to the window so that his face was as dark as theirs were light.

—May I say something first? said the boy.

—Of course, said the commissaire.

Graham was frightened. He did not want the boy to speak. He thought:

—He's going to try and excuse me, to ask them to be lenient with me. I don't want that. I did what I did and it's over now. I don't want to have to justify it. Besides, they'll just laugh at him, laugh at me. What right has he got to make me look ridiculous?

—What is it you wish to say? the commissaire asked the boy, tapping the passport against his chin.

—It's just that this man . . .

—Ah, yes! Could we have your name, please, monsieur?

—Graham Winter, said Graham, and the young gendarme wrote it down in his notebook.

—This man, continued the boy, he . . . he knew nothing about . . . I told him this story. I said I was hitchhiking. He was just giving me a lift, nothing else. He isn't involved.

There was a moment in which Graham could have spoken. The commissaire looked at him, turned his darkened face toward him and lifted his eyebrows and Graham could have said:

—That isn't true.

But he did not.

He wanted to. He wanted to get the whole business over with but there was something in the commissaire's eyes that stopped him: a message, or rather not a message but an awareness of the fundamental nature of Graham Winter of which Graham Winter himself was not aware.

The commissaire's eyes said:

—All right. I know he's not telling the truth as well as you do. But what is the truth, after all? A matter of words? Of course not. At their least corrupt words are only the compromise that we extend to each other in lieu of understanding. At their worst they're a minefield of trip wires and booby traps designed specifically to keep truth a prisoner.

—I don't believe a thing the boy's saying but that's not important. I do believe that you're innocent. Oh, not technically, legally innocent perhaps, although that may be hard to prove if you chose to stick to this story. Who knows? Merely innocent of being guilty, of being anything.

—I don't know you, Monsieur Graham Winter. I don't

141

know who you are, what you do, or how you came to be involved in this boy's little tragedy, but I have seen you before. You, sitting there with your lips pressed, so aware, even at this moment, that your breath is not as fresh as it should be, you fighting so hard not to weaken yourself by expressing the slightest emotion when you should be fighting for your freedom as the boy is doing for you—I have seen you before. I have seen pathologists dissecting the bodies of old women with flat breasts. I have seen police photographers focusing their expensive lenses on the butchered corpses of whores.

—The boy has gray sweat in the hairs above his top lip. He looks like a second-rate drag act and is pathetic.

—You I do not pity. Nor do I admire you. I feel nothing for you. If I find that you are guilty of being an accessory after the fact I shall arrest you. If there is no real proof I shall let you go. There will probably be no real proof. You will not contradict the boy's story. There are loopholes and people like you cannot help but bend low enough to slip through them.

And Graham said nothing.

The commissaire said:

—So Monsieur Winter was just "giving you a lift." I see. And all this time he believed you to be a woman? Yes?

—Yes. Yes, that's right. You see, I met him in this hotel in Brittany and he said he was coming down here and . . . Well, no, at first he just offered to give me a lift to the train and then he said he fancied going south too. The weather up there was . . .

—We can corroborate all this? With the hotel?

142

—Oh, yes.

—Monsieur Winter?

—Yes.

His voice caught in his throat.

—Yes, he said again, too loud this time.

—The Hotel des Sables at Benmel. Monsieur and Madame Bonnet.

—And what can they tell us? That you knew nothing about Monsieur Howard's criminal activities?

—They can tell you that I'd never seen him before he arrived there, that I . . . that we all thought he was a girl.

—Can they? Why did you run away from the ship yesterday evening, Monsieur Winter?

—What?

—Do you not understand the question?

—Yes. Yes, of course.

—Then?

—Is it important? said the boy. I mean, has it got anything to do with . . . ?

—If Monsieur Winter was merely giving you a lift to Marseilles, then it is interesting to know why, at the last minute, he tried to stop you from leaving the country. Did he, perhaps, have some second thoughts?

—I told you, he didn't know about me. If he'd known, why would he have tried to stop me?

—Why *did* he try to stop you?

—He . . . he just wanted me to stay.

—Why?

The boy hesitated.

By the half-open office window Commissaire Tourot slid

the passport he was holding between the palms of his hands and rubbed its spine along the bridge of his nose. The young gendarme shuffled and coughed. Outside a car changed gear.

—He said he was in love with me, said the boy.

—So? said the commissaire and simultaneously Graham said:

—No!

—He did, said the boy. He did. That's why he didn't want me to leave. Of course, he didn't realize that I . . . I had to tell him then.

—No!

—There is nothing to be ashamed of, Monsieur Winter, said the commissaire. You have assured me that you were not aware of the young gentleman's sex.

—No. No, but . . .

—Well, then? said the commissaire. And to the boy:

—What happened next?

—I told him everything, said the boy, and he tried to persuade me to hand myself in. That's when the police found us, in any case.

—Most convenient, said the commissaire. But this, of course, explains why Monsieur Winter registered no surprise upon hearing this morning that you were a murderer. I understand that now. It had been worrying me, you see. Yes, it had been worrying me a little.

He walked forward from the window so that his features —his thick nose, the bags under his eyes, the heavy bridge of his mouth—were once more illuminated.

—In that case, he said, I think we have no need to keep

144

you any longer, Monsieur Winter. I am sorry that you have been troubled.

He extended his hand toward Graham. The young gendarme closed his notebook and stood to attention.

—Is that all? said Graham.

—I think so. Don't you?

—Well . . .

He stood up, hitting the wooden chair with the back of his calves so that it tottered a moment before coming to rest once more on the linoleum.

—What about . . . What about Mister Howard? he said.

—That'll be a matter for the British police.

—I see. Well . . .

He felt into his pockets.

—The sergeant at the desk will return your belongings to you. And take your address in England. You may well be needed to give evidence.

—Yes.

Graham forced himself to look at the boy.

The boy's face was turned from him. He saw only the thin shoulders, the large, short-nailed hands spread on knees that protruded like a joke from the dirty beige skirt, the legs, the matted yellow hair.

He swallowed and his saliva tasted of vomit.

He said:

—Good-bye.

The boy did not turn.

The young gendarme came toward Graham and opened the door behind him.

—*Par ici, monsieur.*

—Thank you.

He left the office.

At the sergeant's desk he collected his belongings and wrote out his London address in block capitals on a pink form.

16

The car stood where they had left it.

A parking ticket had been inserted under the right-hand windscreen wiper. Graham removed this and threw it to the ground. He was cold and his eyes ached. He opened the door and got into the car, unprepared for the half-full packet of Gauloises on the dashboard, his suitcase where he had left it on the back seat.

He drove from the port. Nobody tried to stop him.

In the town he stopped at a pâtisserie to buy some brioches. He found that he could not swallow them although his stomach was tight with hunger. He looked at his watch. It was half-past ten. He could not believe that the day was so new nor that this was the same day that he—that they: the girl and he, the boy and he—had seen breaking through the cobwebbed skylight of a warehouse.

People passed by him on the pavement. Their clothes were bright and their skins were golden. Graham shivered in the sunlight, rejecting the warmth that they threw out to him. The carnival colors of the shop awnings, of the young girls' skirts, of the tomatoes and melons and grapes and peppers that tumbled from the greengrocers' stalls, irritated him. They violated the holiness of his grief.

He was not yet aware of the fragility of his emotion, nor that its name was not grief.

He returned to the car and began to drive once more, avoiding the area of the gendarmerie. He followed signposts that said "Arles" and "Nîmes" and "Avignon."

He thought:

—This is what I wanted, for it all to be over. And it is.

—But not like that, he thought. It should have been so different.

There had been moments: in their first meetings, when they had walked together along beaches saying nothing and he had thought that perhaps they understood each other and later with the children and even after that, driving through the night to the warm hum of a car engine, when her head had slumped to one side with tiredness and her hair had brushed the shoulder of his sweater. He remembered how she had touched his hand once and said: "I'm sorry" and how silly she had been wanting to swim in that river outside Aurillac and how they had driven together through Provence and her hair had been whipped back from her face by the wind from the open window.

There were other moments that he was already beginning to forget.

He thought:

—Those people out there, queuing up to buy fish for

their Friday lunch, laughing together on their doorsteps, how can they possibly know what I am feeling now?

How could they know and how could he know that the pain inside him was not sorrow for a girl's life but regret for the life of a man?

Graham had reached the outskirts of the town when he saw the man in the blue suit again.

He had slowed down for some traffic lights and as he was idling there, incuriously looking around, he noticed him.

He was standing at a bus stop, not in fact wearing a blue suit this time but still the same man, his bald forehead thrust forward, his pink hands clasped in front of his stomach, his short, plump body tilting from toe to heel. As Graham watched him he turned and their eyes met.

Graham looked instantly away but not before he had seen the man leave the bus stop and begin to run toward him. The traffic lights stayed at red. Then he realized that the man was calling his name:

—Graham Winter! Graham Winter!

He looked round again. The man was knocking at the far window of the car. The lights turned green.

—*Une seconde!* said Graham and indicated by signs that he would draw up round the corner. When he had done this he rolled down the window and leaned out.

—*Qu'est-ce que vous voulez?* he called.

—It is Graham Winter? said the man.

—Yes.

He could not understand why the man spoke English.

—I thought it must be. Saw you around yesterday as a matter of fact.

—Who are you? said Graham.

—My name's Bonham. Alfred Bonham. Art critic. We've met at Tony Bridge's once or twice.

—No, said Graham.

He would not believe it. This was the man from the supermarket, the detective.

—You probably won't remember me. Such crowded affairs, Tony's parties. But it's my job to remember names. And faces. How's your . . . how's Miranda by the way?

—Miranda? said Graham.

Still he did not understand. This man had watched him in a supermarket, had followed him, had been there at the port the night they . . .

—Is she well? I see she's not with you.

—Miranda? Oh, no. She got married a few months ago. Didn't you know?

—That's right. I heard. I'm so sorry.

—Look here . . . , said Graham.

He wanted to get away. He had made a mistake. This man was not who he had thought he was.

—Oh, I say, I didn't mean to hold you up, old boy, but as a matter of fact I wonder if you could do me a small favor.

—Of course, said Graham.

—Well, it's just that I'm trying to get into Aix for lunch with some friends of mine who have a villa there and not being able to drive I'm rather at the mercy of these ghastly

150

continental buses. I wondered if by any chance you were going in that sort of direction . . .

—I'm going to Brittany, said Graham. I have some things to collect and this car . . . it's not mine . . . Oh, I'm sorry. I . . . No. Yes, of course you can have a lift.

—Is it dreadfully out of your way?

—Not at all.

He released the lock on the door. The man got in.

—It's not a Rolls, said Graham.

—No, said the man. Not quite.

—Look here, said Graham. This may sound odd but you weren't in a supermarket in town yesterday, were you? About lunchtime?

—As a matter of fact, yes, said the man. I didn't think you'd recognized me.

—I'm awfully sorry. I . . . And at the port, last night. You were there too, weren't you? Weren't you?

—I . . .

—You were standing by a fence. You . . . I remember you spoke to a sailor.

—Really!

—I've got to know.

—I can't see that . . . Yes, I was there. I might have been there. Look, do you mind if I ask what this third degree's all about?

—What? said Graham.

—Oh, nothing. I . . . It's not important.

He narrowed his eyes to read a signpost.

After a while the man said:

151

—Alone, are you?

—Yes, said Graham. Yes, I am.

—What is it? A working holiday? Are you about to aston-ish us with some more of your charming little landscapes?

—Yes, said Graham. Well, I mean I've done a bit of painting. Nothing much.

—Don't say that. There are so few painters nowadays who seem to care about beauty.

He sighed.

—Yes, he said. I was sorry to hear about you and Miranda. Still, I daresay it's all for the best.

—What do you mean?

—Well, you know, she was quite a tough lady, wasn't she? Knew what she wanted. A bit too strong for you, I'd have thought. I don't mean any disrespect, of course, but she was very much a woman of the world, wasn't she?

—I suppose so, said Graham.

—Well, you know what I mean. What a lovely view! No wonder you do so much of your work here. Yours wasn't the happiest of relationships, was it?

—No, said Graham. No, I suppose not. Look, you couldn't light me one of those cigarettes, could you? Help yourself if you like.

He spoke to stop himself from crying.

But after a few miles he could no longer have cried had he tried to. The road was like a white ribbon before him and along the banks thyme and lavender grew. Geraniums hazed the air. The sky stretched blue above him. And when he had dropped Alfred Bonham off at his friends' villa in Aix he drove on alone to Arles, where he found a hotel and

152

had bourride and pork in garlic sauce and a bottle of Châteauneuf-du-Pape.

He also bought a postcard, which he sent to his agent, telling him to expect him back soon.

"I've done one or two nice enough paintings," he wrote. "I hope you like them. I'm feeling very well. The weather here is divine."

73 74 75 76 77 10 9 8 7 6 5 4 3 2 1